ROGUE ENFORCER

INTERSTELLAR BRIDES® PROGRAM
BOOK 22

GRACE GOODWIN

GET A FREE BOOK!

JOIN MY MAILING LIST TO BE THE FIRST TO KNOW OF NEW RELEASES, FREE BOOKS, SPECIAL PRICES AND OTHER AUTHOR GIVEAWAYS.

http://freescifiromance.com

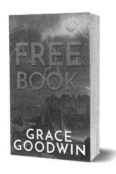

FIND YOUR INTERSTELLAR MATCH!

YOUR mate is out there. Take the test today and discover your perfect match. Are you ready for a sexy alien mate (or two)?

VOLUNTEER NOW!
interstellarbridesprogram.com

1

Abigail "Abby" Gregg, Interstellar Brides Processing Center, Miami, Florida

The slow, heavy movement of a large—make that huge—cock pumping in and out of my body made me gasp and reach for my mate.

I groaned with pleasure as the male fucking me took my hands and shoved them over my head, his heat enveloping me as he fucked me harder. Deeper. Faster.

"Bite me," I begged. The voice was desperate, female, but definitely not mine. My body was too big, too tall, my legs too long. I'd had sex against the wall before, and I knew my legs were not long enough to wrap around a man whose hips were this big. He was big all over. Massive chest lined with sculpted muscle. Thighs as thick as a football player's. Even his hands were bigger than anything I'd ever seen before, easily trapping my wrists between his fingers as he held me in place for his attention.

He thrust deeper, my—her—pussy stretching as our lover tilted his hips, lifting her—me—higher off the ground.

"Patience, mate." His voice was a deep rumble, one this body recognized. Every cell in this body reacted to the sound with anticipation. Heat. My—her—pussy tight. So fucking tight. Ready to explode.

"Now. Please, do it now." The words seemed to drive the male a bit mad as his cock actually swelled inside me, getting bigger. Harder.

Hands over my head, my back was pressed to a hard surface as he shifted his hips, moving in a circular motion until the body I was inhabiting moaned in surrender. I was right there, on the edge with her. I wanted to come. Needed to come. We were soooo close, but I—she—knew we were missing something. Something fucking spectacular. And she wanted it. Badly.

Now.

"Please."

With a grunt, the male before me smiled. I couldn't quite make out his face, his features a bit of a blur. Dark hair? Thick lips? Maybe. What I could see were fangs. Long. Sharp. Dripping with some kind of...venom?

In a panic, I tried to pull back, but the body I was in did the opposite, dropping her—our—head to one side to give this freak better access.

He was going to bite me! And this body *wanted* him to.

Holy shit. What the actual hell was happening right now?

I tried to shout out in protest as the male lowered his head toward my—her—neck. He scraped the sharp points over her sensitive skin, the slight sting making my —her—pussy clench in anticipation. The first shocking stirring of an orgasm rocketed through me in a single spasm. Stopped.

Her moan of protest matched what I was feeling. The orgasm rode me, teased me, wouldn't quite come for a visit. Damn it.

"I want them deep. Fuck me. Bite me. I need you." The female voice sobbed with need. She was desperate. Shameless. I would never beg like that.

Never.

The male fucking me shuddered at her words, his fangs returning to press along the curve of her neck. "You are mine. My mate. I will kill anyone who touches you."

"Yes," she begged, his words, his threat of violence, making her body spin out of control. She was dizzy. Which meant *I* was dizzy. I felt like I was falling. Spinning. Lost.

"Mine."

Fangs sank deep, the shock wave of heat, the momentary flash of pain followed by intense bliss as hot liquid— the best fucking drug I had ever even dreamed existed— flooded my body. My mind. Love exploded inside my—

her—body as her mate claimed her, filled her with his essence.

I had no idea how I knew what was happening, but *she* knew. He was giving her everything. His body. His life. His loyalty. His soul was in that bite. And she took it like the greedy bitch she was—took it all. Leaving nothing for me.

Her body exploded, the orgasm making her wail in a long, drawn-out scream of pleasure that I felt with every cell in my body.

Fuck. Me. My body rocked up off the table as the strange sound of my own voice filled my ears and the male, his bite, the complete and utter bliss I'd been feeling, faded away like a dream.

"No!" I tried to get him back. I wasn't finished. She wasn't finished. We wanted more. I knew she was going to get more. A lot more.

"Miss Gregg? Can you hear me?"

"No."

A soft huff of laughter answered my denial. "Glad you are back in the land of the living. Your testing is complete."

"Send me back." I rolled my head from side to side, testing the hardness of the strange indentation my skull rested between. And then I remembered all of it. The Interstellar Brides testing center. The chair that looked like my worst nightmare from too many visits to the dentist's office—I had a rather terrible sweet tooth when I was young and too many cavities to count. I remembered, too, that my two best friends in the world were gone, really gone. No longer on Earth, gone. Which was just one more layer to the reasoning behind my decision to volunteer as a bride.

That, and I wanted an Atlan warlord like Tane for my very own. Or Bahre. Hell, I wasn't picky. Any warlord would do as long as he looked at me the way Tane looked at my friend Elena. Lucky, lucky Elena. But...Atlans didn't bite. Did they?

I opened my eyes to see a kind but not smiling Warden Egara looking at me with her lips tight and her head tilted at an angle as she studied me. "Are you all right?"

Was I? Well, my body was still pulsing with the after-shocks from an orgasm that hadn't really been mine. I'd been bitten by some kind of freak alien with fangs and loved it. Wanted more. My wrists were in restraints so I wouldn't fall off the chair as I writhed and begged some unknown alien to pump his cock into me, bite me, and make me scream. And I had no idea what the hell I'd just seen. I'd signed up to get matched to an Atlan. Not...that. Whatever that alien creature had been.

"I don't like vampires. You know that, right?" The thought of sucking blood had always made me nauseous. Gross. Just gross.

Warden Egara raised her perfectly arched brow. "There are no vampires in the Coalition Fleet."

"Then what's with the fangs?"

She glanced down at the tablet screen she held in her

hands. "You have been matched to the moon base Rogue 5. The people there are hybrid descendants of a native race of fanged creatures who lived on the planet Hyperion."

"All of them? They all have fangs?"

"Yes." She studied me for long, silent seconds. "Did you find the bite uncomfortable?"

I couldn't lie. I wanted to, but I couldn't make myself do it. "No."

"Excellent." She seemed to breathe a sigh of relief as she ran through a series of rapid-fire questions. Was I married? Did I have children? Was I legally responsible for any children here on Earth? I would have thirty days to reject the match. Blah. Blah. Blah. I'd already read everything, checked every box, and answered all these questions more than once. I barely listened. I couldn't stop thinking about those fangs. That orgasm. That feeling of being blissed out.

That kind of pleasure would be addictive. I'd be eager. Desperate. Needy. I hated that. What if he said no? What if he got her—me—all hot and bothered and needy and then refused to bite me? I would *not* be like that woman in my dream. I would not beg. Would. Not.

"Why do they bite? What's in that venom?"

"It's not venom, my dear. It's a special enzyme complex that promotes healing and helps the males bond with their mates." She grinned at me. "To be honest, I'm not exactly sure how it works. I haven't studied it in detail as you are the first bride I am sending to them."

"What?"

"Well, technically, they are not part of the Coalition Fleet. However, some members of their legions have helped us, so those males qualify for a bride on a case-by-case basis. And this is a very good match. Very good."

"What does that mean?"

"Ninety-eight percent compatible. Nearly perfect."

Perfect? Except I did not like vampires. I'd watched a Dracula movie when I was seven and never moved past it. Even the sparkling vampires that were so popular for a while couldn't erase that dark terror from my memories. "Helped how?"

She shrugged. "Spying, probably. Smuggling. The legions are, technically, criminal organizations. They are run somewhat like our motorcycle gangs, or maybe like the Mafia here on Earth. I'm not exactly sure. But whatever they do for us, I know the I.C. doesn't want their activities in the official records."

"The I.C.?"

"The Intelligence Core. Kind of like your CIA"

God. What had I gotten myself into? "And you're telling me I'm matched to one of these smuggler spy criminals?" Instead of an Atlan? I wanted to cry, but I couldn't quite get over the bliss of that bite. I was losing my mind and all good sense. Officially. Gone.

"Yes. You will be sent to Transport Station Zenith, where your mate will meet you and create a cover story for you."

"Cover story?"

"Outsiders are not allowed on Rogue 5. But don't worry. I know there are at least two other human women mated to members of the legions."

"But not brides."

"Correct. One met her mate at a bar, of all places." Warden Egara laughed. "A space bar called a canteen. She was a medical officer in the Fleet, and from what I hear, they didn't even make it to their room."

Sex in a bar? In space? God. "And the other woman?"

"Oh, she was a fighter. She left the Coalition and infiltrated the legion to avenge her ReCon unit. Her friends were all killed by an overdose of a drug one of the legions sold to her friends."

What? "Did she get them?"

"Her new mate did. Or rather, his legion. I'm not sure exactly what happened. I only get bits and pieces sometimes. Earth is so very far away, after all."

"Gossip will always find a way." I knew that to be one hundred percent fact. Truth or lies, nothing traveled faster than a juicy bit of gossip. What would my social media followers think—all five million of them—if they knew I was going off to be married to a space criminal? What did I think? This mate of mine didn't sound like a big teddy bear Atlan. Or even one of the uptight, rule-following Prillon guards I'd met at the Bachelor Ball or at Chet's house after. I was matched to a criminal? A bad guy?

No. A spy. Maybe like a double agent? Was he a good guy?

Had to be, right? On a case-by-case basis? He'd helped, earned a bride, so he had to be good.

Shit. What if he wasn't? Would I care? That bite had made me lose my mind. Would I care what he did when he wasn't making me sob with out-of-control orgasms?

Damn. Yes. The answer was yes. I would care. "What happens if I don't like him?"

"You have thirty days to decide. If you find Cormac does not make you happy..."

Cormac. His name was Cormac.

"...report to Styx, the leader of his legion. He knows how to contact someone who can get you out of there."

"Okay." At least I had an out. That made me feel better.

"Oh, one more thing. This is a special case. Normally, your mate would be waiting for you with bells and whistles. If you were going anywhere else, I wouldn't have been able to tell you his name. In this case, the Styx legion's involvement with the Coalition Fleet is top secret. Revealing their connection to us could endanger multiple lives. No one can know you are an Interstellar Bride."

"But...how am I supposed to explain being there?"

"Cormac will take care of that, I'm sure. When you arrive, play along. Pretend you know him, that you met him somewhere else. Be vague until you two get your story straight. He will do the same."

Great. Was she serious? I studied her facial features. Not one hint of a teasing grin. No smile. She was deadly serious.

The warden's fingers flew over her tablet, and she seemed to be making multiple selections. "I do believe you are ready to go."

"I—"

A line appeared in the wall next to me, and the chair I was sitting on jolted to the side as it moved into the new space the retreating section of wall created. Beyond the wall was a room bathed in blue light with a small pool in its center.

"Hold still, Abby. You need your NPU."

I knew from dealing with the Atlan Warlords and from my own research that the Neural Processing Unit was some kind of universal translator. I wouldn't be able to understand my new mate or anyone else in space without it. Holding perfectly still, I waited as a slender robotic arm moved toward my head. The sharp tip settled just below and behind my ear. I winced as it pierced my skin. This bite hurt a hell of a lot more than the vampire man's had in my dream. Vision? Memory?

"Wait! What does he look like?" I squirmed in the stupid hospital-style gown I was wearing, my bare backside sticking to the seat, my thighs and bottom coated with my arousal. I was very ready for some hot sex. Really hot sex. With a vampire criminal.

What the hell was going on here? Was there something wrong with me? Why didn't I get matched to an Atlan? I really, really wanted an Atlan warlord. Damn it.

I tried to use my arms to shift my weight on the seat but didn't get far. My wrists were restrained, supposedly so I wouldn't fall off and injure myself while I was out of my mind having sex on another planet—in someone else's body. The thought made me squirm even more. I had to stop moving before I got a rug burn. Seat burn. Whatever.

Warden Egara was watching me, and she hadn't answered my question.

"Well?" I insisted. "How am I supposed to know who he is?"

"Normally, I'm not allowed to show you. But this is a bit of an unusual match, so I will. As I said, his name is Cormac. He is a member of Styx legion." She moved her hands even faster over the tablet. Seconds later, the wall before me turned into a large screen.

And there he was. Holy crap. I didn't know when they'd taken the picture, but he didn't look happy. His eyes were dark and narrowed as if he were annoyed. His hair was so short it looked like a buzz cut the army gave new military recruits. I thought maybe it was black as well, but it was nearly impossible to tell the color with it being so short. His face was older. Somber. He looked like he had been to hell and back and could teach a class on cruelty.

But his lips were full. His jaw was cut. He was handsome in a brutal way that made my pussy clench and my nipples grow hard. He wouldn't treat me like a porcelain doll that might break at any moment. No. He looked like the kind of man—alien—who would shove me up against a wall, bite me, and fuck my brains out.

I shuddered with anticipation, with a raw hunger I'd never before allowed myself to feel, as I studied the barely visible tips of his fangs peaking at me from between his lips.

So this was my mate. My hard as nails, take no prisoners, no bullshit mate. Cormac. Cormac with fangs.

I wanted him to bite me. Fill me with his cock and claim me. Like, now. Right freaking now.

Maybe I didn't need an Atlan warlord after all. I'd met several, and not one had made me want to rip his clothes off and demand sex.

Warden Egara waved her hand at me as the chair lowered me, gown and all, into the warm, blue water. I had to admit, the bath felt heavenly. Soothing. So relaxing.

"Good luck, Abby!"

I tried to smile, but I was suddenly so very tired. My eyelids were so heavy.

The last thing I remembered was Warden Egara's voice.

"Your processing will begin in 3...2...1..."

2

Cormac of Styx Legion, Moon Base Rogue 5

Enforcer. The word made my blood sing with purpose, with my place in the universe. I hunted. I punished. I killed our enemies. I served our people the only way I knew how, and I was very good at my job.

Killing had become too easy.

"You cannot hide from me, Siren scum." I yelled the truth to the male I sensed cowering just ahead. Twenty paces and I'd be on top of him, my Styx legion armor specialized to deflect an ion blast. He would have no choice but to fight me in hand-to-hand combat. One on one.

Or surrender and face my leader, Styx himself, for judgment.

Neither option would end well for this fucker. He'd attacked one of our delivery vehicles, tried to steal our cargo and had injured our pilot badly enough that he was currently unconscious in a ReGen pod.

Maintenance lights lined the corridor. The sickly green glow added to the resignation flooding my body with every step. I did not enjoy killing, but I accepted that protecting the legion was necessary to our survival. I did what needed to be done.

The sound of grinding machinery filled the cold air with a distinct metallic hum. Condensation dripped from the walls, created by water vapor leaking into the area from the filtration and waste recyclers. The bowels of the shipping port on this side of the moon were colder than the rest. This area was not heated to accommodate Rogue 5's inhabitants. Instead, it was kept just warm enough to prevent the water and machines from freezing. No energy was wasted in space. It was too fucking difficult to survive out here. The Coalition Fleet was too busy fighting their war to spare resources for us. For centuries we'd been left to fend for ourselves.

Weary to the bone, I forced my boots to move forward through the dim corridor beneath the docks. I had a job to do, and I would complete the mission my brother Styx had given me, or I would not return to him. That was my way and the reason every member of our legion stepped aside and dropped their gaze when I entered a room. None but my legion's top-ranking members would dare speak to me. The thought made me grunt with disgust at the others for their cowardice and at myself for the hurt that wormed through my heart like a parasite.

Ignoring the pain, as I had since I was old enough to remember, I checked my scanners. There. Three corners down. A heat signature on the left. It was faint, but I knew the Siren legion smugglers had the most advanced body armor and weapons they could steal. If not for his need to breathe, I'd have nothing to go on but instinct.

Even that would have been enough. The ancient Everian Hunter in my ancestry had given me certain gifts. Combined with my Prillon and Hyperion blood, I had the loyalty of a warrior, the instincts of an Elite Hunter and the savagery of the Hyperion race that gave me the fangs I felt breaking free, fully extending in anticipation of battle.

"Siren!"

"Fuck off, Cormac. Don't make me kill you." An ion blast hit the floor and exploded a few steps in front of me.

I knew that voice, knew the male I hunted was as dangerous and deadly as I. "You want to start a war, Shade?" I stopped walking and lifted my blaster to take aim at the corner, waiting for him to show himself. Fuck it all, I didn't want to kill this particular male.

"I didn't kill your pilot."

"He's in a pod."

"He isn't dead."

Shade had a point. He could have killed our pilot during that attack. He'd chosen not to. The male had honor, and he had proven it many times over the years I had known him. "Why the fuck are you still with Siren legion?"

"Someone's got to do it." Shade stepped out from behind the corner, and I held myself steady, blaster raised, but I didn't pull the trigger. "There are children, Cormac. Females. Elders. You know what it is to protect your people."

I did. Fuck it all. Shade was like me, an enforcer for his legion. He just happened to work for the most vile, evil bitch on all of Rogue 5. Siren had no moral compass, no honor. She was ruthless, cruel and ambitious.

Shade lifted his helmet off his head and stared at me. "You going to kill me, or can we both pretend you never saw me and get the fuck out of here before we freeze to death?"

"If you'd killed him, you'd be dead." I lowered my blaster as my comm alerted me to an incoming message. "Cormac."

The comm device implanted behind my ear buzzed as the transmission came in. "Cormac. This is Styx. You have to get to Transport Station Zenith right fucking now." My adopted brother, Trace, now known as Styx, the leader of our legion, sounded worried. And Styx never fucking sounded worried.

Ignoring Shade, I turned back the way I'd come, already breaking into a run. "What's happening?"

"You've been matched to an Interstellar Bride."

I skidded to a stop. "What?" Confusion swamped me. The words he'd spoken did not make sense. Impossible.

"Listen to me. You have an Interstellar Bride. That Prillon fucker, Helion, put you in their system, remember?"

I did. Vaguely. But that had been years ago. I'd long since believed the so-called *processing* I'd gone through had been another empty promise from another asshole. I'd played along because it had been what was best for the legion back when my brother and I were both Enforcers, running wild and causing problems. Before he'd become Styx. Before he'd met his mate, a human female named Harper from a planet none of us had heard of at the time. I recalled the matching process clearly. On my brother's insistence, I had allowed Helion himself to shove me into a chair and sedate me, and then I had dreamed about sex, about gifting a female my bite and my venom as my cock was buried deep, as my seed pumped into her body. To be fair, the vision had been more intense than anything I'd ever experienced before or since. I'd woken up covered in my own cum, ready to kill Helion for pulling me away from an imaginary female.

That female was a ghost. She had never been real. And no fucking female was going to want me for more than a hot, dirty ride. I had years of experience and solid evidence to prove that truth. I was the monster they fucked in an alley, not the male they chose for a mate, to be a father to their children.

"That was years ago. And I don't trust that Prillon." I'd thought the entire matching process a cruel joke. But still,

I'd never been able to stop thinking about it. Not for one fucking day. Helion had given me a private hell to suffer. More than once I'd considered hunting that Prillon down and ending him.

"No one trusts him. But he gets things done."

"If neither one of us trusts him, what the fuck are we talking about?" I was running again. I was at least thirty minutes from the boundary of Styx territory. Officially, the docks were neutral ground, but I didn't want to talk about the work we'd done for Dr. Helion or the Coalition Fleet's Intelligence Core anywhere outside the safety of Styx legion's protected meeting spaces where our technology—and our well-armed guards—kept things private.

"Cormac, brother, stop moving and hear what I am telling you."

I did as he commanded. Always. Styx was the only living soul who had my complete and total loyalty. He'd fucking earned it.

My feet stilled. I took a deep breath. Gods be damned. This was insane. Had to be a cruel joke. "I am listening."

Styx sighed. "You, Cormac of Styx legion, have been matched to a female with a ninety-eight percent compatibility rating. She's yours, your perfect match. She is your mate, an Interstellar Bride. As we speak, she is being transported from Earth—"

"She is human?" Styx's mate was human. Harper. An excellent female. I felt the first stirrings of hope and hated the feeling immediately, shoving it back down.

"Yes. And right now, she is in the middle of transport. She will arrive at TSZ in the next few hours. And if you aren't there to claim her—"

"Fuck." TSZ was short for Transport Station Zenith, a Coalition-controlled space station frequented by every type of criminal, killer and scum out here on the edges of space, including members of the other legions—our enemies. They would love to get their hands on a female from Styx legion, doubly so if she were mine. I had made many enemies over the years.

"Exactly. Get back here. I have them fueling my ship in our private dock. Fastest thing we've got. It will be ready when you arrive."

"I am on my way." I would need to fly directly to the station. Rogue 5's legions had made navigating the labyrinth of asteroids, space mines and gravity wells impossible for outsiders. The natural energy fields surrounding Hyperion and the moon base we lived on made using transport impossible. The only way in or out of Rogue 5's solar system was to fly.

I looked down at myself. I was covered in dust and grime, armed to the teeth with dark hunting paste covering my face and neck in a pattern I'd learned years ago that confused the eye. I'd been hunting. Now, with my new mate in danger, I didn't have time to clean up and look like a prince when I greeted her.

My *mate*. How was this possible? But my brother would not lie to me. Ever. And never about something as sacred as a mate.

My pulse sped, and my cock stirred at the thought of having a female of my own. The processing dream from all those years ago swirled in my mind, and my fangs descended. Ached. Eager to bite. Bury my cock deep. Claim a mate.

First, I would see to her safety. Then I would worry about my appearance. It wasn't like she would want to fuck me the moment we met. It would most likely take months of wooing her, of slow seduction, to convince her I would never harm her. Females and children—fuck, even the males in our legion—kept a safe distance from me. This female, my *perfect match,* must be fierce. She would probably be muscular and strong. Tall. Perhaps a soldier from Earth. That would make sense, a female who would not fear me nor be taken aback by my appearance, my duties or my past.

She would be stern. Hardened. Wise. Fearless. A warrior like me.

My mate would be perfect.

3

Abby, Transport Station Zenith

My head spun, the dizziness so total I didn't dare move. I was lying on something cold and hard that felt like metal. I pressed my forehead down and took a few deep breaths, trying to make the floor beneath me stop moving.

This was like motion sickness on top of food poisoning when I already had the flu. Thank god my stomach was empty.

I didn't know if I stayed there for one minute or ten, but eventually I noticed the same cold metal pressed to my thighs, my hip, my nipples. I was naked.

Why the hell was I naked?

Shocked into movement, I opened my eyes and tried to push up off the floor. Everything dipped and spun, and

I collapsed onto my side, panting, swallowing the gag reflex swelling in my throat. I didn't have any idea when I'd eaten last. I didn't know what day it was. The last thing I remembered was that blue water, Warden Egara's voice, then falling asleep.

Now...this.

"My lady?" A deep, resonant voice vibrated inside my skull like my head was a gong.

"Are you talking to me?" I whispered my question, concentrating on the cold pressed to my cheek.

"Indeed." Moments later, something large and soft was draped over me like a blanket. Maybe it was a blanket. I didn't open my eyes to look. If I looked, I'd have to acknowledge whoever this was had just seen me naked. Groggy. Gagging. My hair probably looked like greasy straw, and I doubted I had my usual carefully applied makeup in order. My armor. I felt like a weakling. Scared. Sick. Whining like a baby.

Pathetic.

Oh, shit. What if the guy who'd covered me up was my mate? My Cormac? And I was making a fool of myself? Great way to start.

I opened my eyes, a soft groan escaping me as the light pierced them like toothpicks shoved deep. I squinted against the pain and looked at the alien—totally freaking *alien*—who was kneeling within arm's reach. Skin the color of burnished gold, angular features, eyes like yellow diamonds. He did not have short, dark hair. No haunted, intense eyes. No fangs.

Nope. This guy was a Prillon. Big and handsome? Yes. But not mine. Not. Mine.

I wanted my man, my mate, the one guaranteed to care about me and put me first. I'd never had that from a boyfriend, never even from a best friend, until Elena and Dominique had shown me what real friendship could be. I'd never had it from my father. My mom? She'd been amazing, but she was dead. Gone. For years. I was tired of being alone and ignored by the people I loved and loved by people who had no idea who I truly was. I had millions of followers on social media back home. Some of them said they loved me. But they had no idea what they were talking about. They loved a mirage. A fantasy. The person I pretended to be in order to make them happy.

My entire life was lies and games and illusion. I was tired of pretending. Cormac was going to be the first real lover I'd had in my life. This Prillon didn't matter to me. Only Cormac.

"I have summoned the doctor. You transported a vast distance, and you are very small."

Oh no, he did *not* just use my size as a reason for weakness. A boy in school once laughed at me when I was so furious I wanted to rip his head off his shoulders and dance in the shower of his blood. He'd grinned, said I was three hundred pounds of sass in a hundred-pound body and informed me I was cute when I was mad.

Cute.

Fuck cute. Fuck this rolling nausea. Fuck this headache. I was tired of being cute. I shoved up into a sitting position and fought tooth and nail to remain upright. I succeeded. "Where is Cormac?"

The Prillon studied me for long seconds before smiling. "You're from Earth, aren't you? A human female?"

"Yes. What difference does that make?"

His smile turned into a chuckle as another Prillon, this one with skin the color of copper and eyes like dark coffee, knelt next to him and extended his arm to hold a glowing green wand over me. "I am Doctor Benten. Human females have developed a reputation in the Fleet." This new male, the doctor, wore a dark green uniform and was smiling as well.

"What kind of reputation?" Sitting fully, I wrapped the blanket around me like a tent and put my legs into a crisscross to help steady me as the doctor paused with the green wand near my temple. The nausea and headache improved noticeably in the span of a few seconds. I couldn't stop the sigh of relief when the pain faded completely and my stomach settled.

"Better?" the doctor asked.

"Yes. Thank you." Wow. I really needed to get one of those green wand things. Maybe Cormac would have one. Surely he would if these Prillons did.

The doctor remained kneeling, keeping himself low enough that I didn't have to crane my neck to speak to him. Trouble was, I didn't want to talk to him. I wanted my mate. I wanted clothes. I wanted to feel safe and protected and like I belonged somewhere.

"Where is Cormac? He's from Styx legion. Do you know where he is?"

The Prillon doctor's dark eyes narrowed. "How do you know him?"

Oh no. Warden Egara said I had to lie. Scratch that. She'd told me Cormac would be here waiting for me and we would pretend to know each other. No one was supposed to know I was an Interstellar Bride, or the whole spy thing Styx legion was doing for the Intelligence Core would be exposed, and I would put my new mate in danger. So where was he?

"I—"

Before I could finish making up a plausible story, a sliding door opened, and the biggest, scariest bastard I'd ever seen stomped into the room like he was going to kill everyone inside. He was huge, his shoulders at least twice as wide as mine. Legs like tree trunks. He was covered head to toe in some kind of armor in shades of gray and black, and a silver band wrapped around his upper arm on one side. Worse, he was covered in gadgets and weapons I had never seen before. I recognized a large, serrated blade as a dagger, and he had a shiny silver space pistol as well as a huge rifle strapped across his back.

"No weapons in transport. I don't care what legion you're from. You know the rules." The golden Prillon stood between the giant and me, blocking my view. I leaned to the side, peeking around his legs to study the markings the intruder had painted onto his face and neck in a pattern that looked like something I'd once seen in a documentary about Navy SEALs who camouflaged their skin when they were on a mission. Was this terrifying alien on some kind of military operation? And why was my entire body suddenly on high alert, code red, heart pounding, mouth gone dry?

I licked my lips as I stared at the strongest, most frightening being I had ever seen—and that was saying something because I knew some Atlans back on Earth. The beasts didn't make my pulse race or my breasts grow heavy. I'd never once wanted to run to one of the warlords and rip his clothes off to discover if the muscles I could see under their armor were real.

The intruder's gaze locked on my lips, and I ran my tongue over them again, unable to stop myself from taunting the monster. The pulse at the base of his neck sped up to match mine as his gaze narrowed.

A low rumble emanated from his throat, and the two Prillons shifted into more fluid stances, their knees bent, the golden one wielding his weapon as if expecting an attack.

The doctor had also placed himself in front of me, one hip turned toward the back of the room where he held his hand over his own space pistol. The other hand he held out, palm open as if he could ward off the threat.

A doctor with a gun? What was this, the Wild West?

"Get the fuck away from my mate." The intruder ignored the golden Prillon's space gun and locked his gaze with mine. "Are you unharmed?"

Mate? Did he just say mate?

Oh. My. God. This...animal, this monster, this scary alien armed to the teeth and covered in war paint was my mate? "Cormac?" My pulse went from pounding to frantic in less than a second.

The green wand the doctor had placed back into a loop on his green uniform beeped some kind of alarm, the light going from green to yellow. He glanced from me to Cormac. "You are scaring her. Her pulse rate is too high."

The doctor turned around and pulled out the wand. "My lady, you need to calm down."

"Get the fuck away from my female." Cormac's order reverberated around the room. "I will take care of her. Get out."

"But—" the doctor tried to argue.

"Get the fuck out. Both of you before I claim my rights under Coalition law and kill you both."

I froze, literally froze. What was I supposed to do? I was sitting on the floor, naked. This male, this alien, was supposed to be mine. Mine.

The Prillons looked as if they were going to risk the fight. Shit. I couldn't let these alpha male idiots kill each other over me. Jeez. What would a real wife do? One who knew her husband the way I was supposed to already know Cormac?

I had no idea. But I had to try something. I cleared my throat to get their attention.

"Cormac, it's okay. They didn't hurt me. The doctor

was treating me because I was sick and dizzy after transport and you were late." I glared right back at the big brute. "I expected you to be here when I arrived." There. I put some sass on that last bit, chastising him for scaring the crap out of me—and for being *late*. For not being here. For not putting me first. Again. Why was this happening to me again?

"I was hunting."

That was supposed to be an apology? Oh no he didn't. I'd spent too many hours waiting for my father while he worked and worked and broke promise after promise. All that old hurt surged to the surface, and I had to fight back tears. "Hunting for what? Your manners? I landed on this transport pad naked and sick, and this Prillon doctor had to take care of me. It should have been you." *Why wasn't it you?*

The golden Prillon stiffened and risked a glance over his shoulder at me. I ignored him and his shocked grin, glaring at my *mate.*

Cormac looked at the doctor. "Is she well enough to travel?"

The doctor glanced at his green wand thing. "Yes. I believe so. But she will be tired and hungry. Transport is more difficult for humans than it is for us."

Cormac dipped his chin to acknowledge the doctor, then strode toward me. The Prillons both moved aside as he reached me. He knelt and scooped me up off the floor, the blanket the Prillon had covered me with wrapped around me like I was a burrito.

"We were unaware you had a mate and were only trying to protect her. Apologies, Enforcer." The golden Prillon sounded sincere.

Cormac grunted. "Speak of this to no one. I do not want her to become a target before I can get her off this station."

"Of course," the doctor agreed. "You should know, there is a full contingent of Siren members on level nine."

"And Cerberus?" Cormac asked. I had no idea who any of these people were, so I stayed quiet in Cormac's arms. It was like being carried around by a giant tree with arms of solid wood. Everything about him was hard. Unforgiving. Powerful.

I'd never felt safer, which shocked me as much as it made me eager to get him naked. He was mine. Right? He would never hurt me, never leave me, never ignore me or forget I existed. Mine. And I was his. I finally belonged somewhere. With someone.

"Less than five of Cerberus legion onboard. Since the new leader took over, they have not been as much of a problem."

Without another word, Cormac walked toward the sliding doors. He paused there and pulled the blanket up to cover my face and head.

"Hey!"

"You will remain hidden until we reach our rooms. We will remain on the station until the repairs are complete on Styx's ship."

"Are you serious? I have to hide? For how long?" I

peeked out from under the blanket to find him staring down into my face with those dark, dangerous eyes. My pussy went hot and tight, and my breathing hitched. God, he was lethal to my libido. He was big and dangerous and scary, and I *wanted* him.

"One or two days. Should anyone see you with me on this station, you will have a price on your head simply because you are mine."

"What about on Rogue 5?" I asked.

His grin would have terrified me if he weren't mine. "Here we must abide by Coalition law. On Rogue 5, we are the law. If anyone tries to harm you, they will be eliminated."

"Eliminated? As in you would kill them?"

"Hunt. Torture. Kill. I protect what is mine." He shrugged as if the threat were commonplace.

Holy shit. My entire body reacted with a visceral gut punch of lust that made me tremble. Who was I? Why did his vow make me want to tear his clothes off with a primal scream of power? What was happening to me?

I had no idea. All I knew was he woke me up, made me feel powerful and safe and protected in a way I never had been before. He was big and scary and fucking gorgeous.

A ninety-eight percent match? Hell, yeah. I didn't care what I had to do now.

He was mine, and I was keeping him.

4

Cormac

My cock ached for her as I carried her through the transport station to one of Styx legion's private rooms. The legion had purchased designated quarters on the station so we could install our own security, and so we always had somewhere to go during our frequent trade runs.

As an Enforcer, I rarely left Rogue 5. No doubt my presence on the station had already caused a stir. The last time I'd come to Transport Station Zenith had been to hunt down and kill a merchant who had put a price on my brother's head. I terminated the idiot and all four assassins who had agreed to take the job.

No one threatened Styx legion and survived.

As I carried my new mate through the doorway into

the safety of Styx quarters, I realized the ferocity of my duty to protect my legion paled in comparison to my *need* to protect *her*.

And yet, there had to have been a mistake. This female could not be mine. There was no possibility of our match being nearly perfect. She was small, too small. Fragile. Breakable. And too innocent as well, if the perfection of her face was to be believed. Not one line or scar marred the smooth beauty of her skin. And her eyes? Clear blue pools that had threatened to drop me to my knees. Her hair was like glimmering golden starlight. She was a delicate goddess, and I a monster.

I'd wanted to kill two honorable Prillons simply for being near her.

I never lost control like that.

Never.

This human was dangerous. My brother's mate had calmed him, not enraged him. Since mating to Harper, both my brother and Blade were calmer, more content. They smiled more often. Even laughed once in a while.

So why did the presence of this female make me so agitated I wanted to pound my fist into a wall until I was bloody?

'Hunt. Torture. Kill. I protect what is mine.'

I had spoken the truth and watched her eyes become round with shock. She had trembled with fear in my arms.

How was I going to touch her, fuck her, claim her, if I terrified her?

Gods be damned, she was so small she would break if I took her the way instinct demanded. The thought did nothing to calm my eager cock nor wipe the images of pounding into her pussy from my mind.

Fuck. She was trembling again. My mate was afraid, and all I had done was hold her.

I stood just inside the room, frozen in place as I contemplated what to do next. We would be staying in Styx and Blade's private quarters, the furniture large and soft and covered with pillows. I knew the bedroom to be equally decadent, with a large bed and bathing area large enough for Styx, Blade and their mate, Harper.

Abigail looked around, her golden head peeking out from beneath the blanket I'd used to conceal her face from the many vid monitors on the station. "Is this where we're staying?"

"Yes. These quarters belong to Styx legion. We will be safe here, Abigail."

"Abby. My friends call me Abby." She turned her head to look up at me and my gaze locked with hers. Everything faded. I swayed on my feet, suddenly unsteady.

"Abby." I tried it out, found I liked the sound of her name on my tongue.

She smiled up at me and my cock jumped; the air froze in my throat.

Fuck, I was in trouble. I barely knew her, and already I could not control my body's responses. Would I lose control completely once I fucked her? Or would this burning need subside?

It had to calm. I could not function like this. Would be unable to hunt.

And her face. Her eyes. She looked so...young.

"How old are you?"

Her expression changed instantly, her gaze narrowing, her lips forming a hard, firm line. "Old enough to know what I want."

"That's not an answer. I am too old for you. Too hard. You should choose another male." There. I'd stated the obvious. She had yet to see my face beneath the paint I'd worn on the hunt, the streaks of gray at my temples—not just from age but from the stress of the hunt. She was youth and beauty and innocence. I was pain and consequence. Death.

If she walked away now, I could let her go. Send her back to Earth to be matched to someone worthy in the Coalition Fleet. Someone younger, gentler.

Anyone but me.

"Why would I choose someone else? Warden Egara said we were a nearly perfect match."

"And what if she's wrong?"

"Is that what you think?"

"I don't know. But I am not gentle, Abby. I am cruel. Brutal. Even the people in my legion are frightened of me." She wiggled a bit and I obliged, setting her on her feet, once more shocked at her size. The top of her head barely reached my chest. So small. So fragile. So breakable.

"Is that so?" Abby wandered the room, touching

things, running her hands over the soft fabrics covering the dark furniture. The room was designed for comfort, and already I could imagine spending hours here making Abby mine. I would bend her over the sofa and take her from behind. Settle her in the chair, spread her legs wide and feast on her pussy until she begged me to fuck her. There was a bath large enough for me to hold her in my arms and gently clean every inch of her before taking her again.

And again.

The blanket she wore dropped off one of her shoulders, exposing the skin there, the side of her neck, the upper swell of one small, perfectly formed breast.

My fangs extended, eager to bite the pale curve of her shoulder.

Fuck. I was becoming an animal.

She peeked into the bathing chamber, walked past the kitchen area and ran her fingertips along the edge of the S-Gen machine, the technology we used to create everything we needed to survive from pure energy. Clothing. Food. Everything. She paused, her nose crinkling in a way I immediately found endearing. "Elena told me about these. You can make anything you want, right?" She turned to look up at me.

"Yes."

"And it's programmed with human food, too? Because of the woman mated to Prime Nial?"

"Yes. That is the rumor. I do not know why the Coalition Fleet chooses to program what they do. I am not part of the Coalition, Abby. I am part of a criminal organization that operates in Coalition space."

"Oh, I know. She told me."

"Who?"

"Warden Egara. Back on Earth."

"And that doesn't bother you? The fact that your mate is a smuggler? A hunter? A killer?"

Abby shrugged as if the blood on my hands didn't matter in the slightest. "She said you were some kind of spy or something super-secret. That I couldn't tell anyone I was an Interstellar Bride because it could put you and your legion in danger if anyone knew you guys were helping them."

"Fuck."

She laughed, and the sound made my cock ache. The ignorant idiot single-mindedly wanted to be buried balls deep in her hot pussy, pumping into her body until her orgasm made the walls of her pussy clamp onto us like a fist. Milking us of our seed.

Planting a child in her womb.

My child. Someone who wouldn't be afraid of me every time I looked into their eyes. Someone who would love me regardless of what I could bring to the table. I wouldn't need to kill to be valued. To be worthy. To keep my place.

Only my brother cared about me. To the rest of the legion, I was a necessary evil. A tool to keep order, to protect Styx legion's assets. To kill who needed killing.

I realized I'd been staring at the curve of her breast

and hastened to lift my gaze to her face. I might feel like an animal, but I did not need to behave as one.

"Were you on a mission? Is that why you have all that paint on your face?"

"Yes." I would not tell her I was sent to eliminate a member of another legion. Nor would I tell her I found Shade and allowed him to leave unscathed. No one need ever know. I did it for the females and children of Siren legion. Shade was under the control of a vile bitch, but he was not without honor.

"Okay." She moved toward me, holding my gaze with every step. When she was close enough to touch, she held out her hand. "Come on."

I could no more deny her than stop my own heart from beating. Carefully, I reached for her hand, my much larger hand completely enveloping her. She did not flinch with fear. In fact, she gently tugged me closer. "First, you're going to kiss me. Then we are going to take a shower, or bath, or whatever that thing in there does because I smell like outer space or something weird, and I want to see your face."

Naked with her? Water sliding over her curves? Perhaps she would touch me as well, slide her hands over my body as she bathed the stench of the docks from my body.

Now I trembled. I wanted her. Needed her. Dared to hope she might want me back.

Fuck.

"I won't be able to keep my hands off you, Abby. My

cock is hard as a rock. Has been since I first saw you. I want to fuck you until you scream, and I don't think I can be gentle."

A shudder passed over her body, but this time I smelled the scent of feminine arousal as well. A drop of fluid leaked from the tip of one fang to land on my lower lip.

Abby gasped and lifted her free hand to wipe the drop of my essence, my gift for my mate, from my lip. She raised the wetness to her mouth and slid the wet pad of her fingertip into her mouth. I nearly groaned.

Gods be damned, this female was going to fucking own me.

She pulled her fingertip from her mouth slowly, mimicking what I could imagine she might do to my cock. Sucking me deep. Swallowing my seed. Closing her hot, wet mouth around my length and sucking. Hard.

I held perfectly, utterly still, afraid to move. If I moved, I would have her pushed against the wall, cock buried balls deep before I had time to think.

Control.

Abby stood unmoving as well, her gaze locked with mine. "Do you want me? I mean, do you want to have sex with me?"

"Yes."

"But you're afraid you're going to freak me out? Scare me?"

"Gods, yes."

Her smile was pure seduction. "I'm no virgin, Cormac.

I might be young, but I'm not innocent. Would you like to know how many men I've slept with?"

"No." I would want to kill them all.

"Fourteen."

"I said no." My vision blurred with jealous rage, the Hyperion blood in my body writhing with possession. Obsession. I thought I could let her go. "I can't. No."

She leaned in close, dropped the blanket and pressed her naked body to my filthy armor. "I've had twice that many dicks in my mouth."

"Stop." My fangs swelled, instinct demanding I put my mark on her body, inject her with my essence, heal her, make her come, claim her. Now. Right fucking now.

She would want no one else. Need no one else. I would protect her, fuck her, care for her. Give her pleasure. Kill for her. Die for her.

I could not hold back the soft sound of denial that escaped my pain-filled chest. She was hurting me with her words. With her need. With hope. Fucking terrible hope.

"Not one of those men meant anything to me. Do you understand? They were nothing. Losers I used to try to feel something real." She traced the seams on the chest of my uniform with her fingers. Touching me. Petting me. "You're real, Cormac. And you're mine now." She lifted her arms and wrapped them around my neck, smearing my camouflage paint over her soft skin. Her fingers met and locked together at the base of my skull. She tugged me down toward her, and I did not resist. When my lips were close enough that our breaths mingled, she held my gaze and whispered her vow to me. "You're mine. No one has ever been mine before. Do you understand? Mine. And I'm *never* letting you go. *Never.*"

"Do not make promises you cannot keep, Abby."

"Fuck you, Cormac. You. Are. Mine. You're big and mean and sexy and you're mine."

Something inside me jolted at the boldness in her. The demand.

I lifted her in my arms and took her lips, the kiss far from gentle. This was a reckoning, a plundering, a claiming. The taste of her exploded in my mouth. My cock jumped. My pulse pounded through my body until there was nothing but the constant thudding of need threatening to break me open, make me explode.

Abby's tongue dueled with mine, never relenting, never giving in. A challenge. A dare. Defiance. She lifted her legs and wrapped them around my waist, the heated scent of her hot pussy making me growl, the low rumble something I had never heard before.

I sounded like a wounded thing, something broken.

Hurting.

Fuck.

"Bite me, Cormac. Fill me up and bite me." Abby leaned back and thrust her breasts forward, tilted her head back to expose her neck, her chest. She was offering me everything.

Pre-cum leaked from the tip of my cock as I fought for control.

"I am filthy." How could I touch her like this, covered in war paint and weapons? In the trappings of a killer?

"I don't care. I want you. Now. Like this."

If she'd said anything else, I might have been able to resist.

Fuck. That was a lie. I was going to fuck her. Hard. Deep. Mark her with my fangs.

Abby shifted her hips to move her wet pussy over my uniform, seeking contact. Needing release.

I had to give her one last chance to save herself. I lowered my forehead to hers and took a deep breath, searching for calm. "If I claim you, I will never let you go. I will kill anyone who tries to hurt you or take you away from me. This is your last chance, Abby. Tell me to let you go. Walk away."

5

Cormac

"**W**hat do you mean, walk away?"

"Choose someone else." I held onto my honor by a thread. She was too young, too beautiful, to be with someone like me.

"No." She kissed me, hard and fast.

"Abby—"

"I said no, Cormac. I'm not a child. I know what I want."

"You don't know what I am."

"Yes, I do. You're mine. The rest of the universe can go fuck itself."

The coarse words in her sweet voice snapped my control. Her declaration shredded my soul. She meant every word, her tone adamant. Certain. And I was no saint.

I took her mouth as I carried her to the center of the room and laid her on the plush carpet in front of the sofa. The moment she was free, her hands wandered frantically over my uniform, tugging and pulling at the fabric.

"Off. Take it off."

I ripped at the material with one hand, bracing myself over her with the other as I took her nipple into my mouth. She tried to assist, her small hands pushing at the material on my shoulders, her back arching off the floor as I moved my attention to her other breast, the small mounds nearly perfectly sized for me to suck nearly half of the soft flesh into my mouth.

She tasted like something from a dream. Something too perfect to be real.

I couldn't get enough.

I threw the torn remains of my uniform shirt across the room and leaned down to kiss the undersides of her breasts. Her ribs. Stomach. My hips settled between her legs, the dagger and ion blaster strapped to my thighs pressing into the softness of her inner thighs.

She squirmed, and I moved down her body to lock my hands on her thighs, gently pushing her knees wide so I could see what was mine.

Her pussy glistened with welcome, her arousal filling my head with an explosion of lust that erased all thought from my mind. Instinct took over.

I locked my lips onto her core, pushed my tongue deep, fucking her with my mouth as she bucked in my hold. There was no mercy in my grip. She was mine. This pussy was mine. This wet heat? Mine.

I licked and sucked her clit. Fucked her with my tongue until she came apart, her keening cry like a bolt of lightning going down my spine straight into my cock.

Before the walls of her pussy finished pulsing, I opened my pants, pulled my cock free, and moved up her body, anticipation a physical pain as I held myself at her entrance, gently scraping the tips of my fangs over her neck.

"Mine."

One word and I lunged, fangs and cock in unison, plunging deep into her body, making her mine. Marking her skin. Filling her pussy. Giving in to temptation.

She offered herself, and I was too much of a bastard to let her go.

With a cry I wanted to hear over and over again, Abby wrapped her arms around my head and held me to her, her hips bucking against mine, meeting me thrust for thrust as the pleasure of my bite pushed her into another orgasm.

Her pussy muscles spasmed around my hard length. Hot. Tight. So fucking tight as her orgasm rolled into another. And another. I knew she would not stop coming until I pulled my fangs from her body, until I let her go.

Fuck. I couldn't stop. Didn't want to stop.

My essence poured into her bloodstream, into her cells, my bite marking her, healing her. Making her mine. My scent would be in her very blood. Her skin.

My mate.

She came again, her voice a choked whimper as she said my name.

"Cormac. God. Holy shit."

I was no god, had no resistance when it came to her. Her pleasure engulfed me, and my cock stiffened. Swelled. Release came hard and fast in a painful torment of twisting muscle and raw bliss. I pumped harder as I filled her with my seed. I could not hold my bite as heat swept through me like a fire just beneath my skin. I pulled back my fangs even as I burned. I ached. I had never felt anything like this.

My female sank her tiny teeth into my chest, the bite shooting fire straight to my balls. Gods. I was fucked. Finished.

I wanted her to devour me until I had nothing left.

~

*A*bby

*W*e laid together in a tangle on the floor, both of us panting and limp. He was huge, his weight making it hard to get enough air.

Or maybe my struggle was caused by the gagillion orgasms I'd just had.

God, I was going to have to start jogging or something

because there was no way I would give up more of *this*. Of him.

And the bite? Holy hell. Even better than the dream I'd had at the processing center.

Way better.

Cormac wrapped me in his arms and rolled us until I was sprawled across his chest. His cock was still buried deep, my core pulsing with little aftershocks that felt like they might never stop.

I lifted one hand and looked at my palm. It was covered in smears of whatever paint Cormac had on his face and neck. So were my arms. I grinned, figuring I probably had the smears on my face from kissing him... and on my breasts, my stomach and my thighs from him kissing *me*.

Mentally shrugging because I really didn't care if we were a total mess, I placed my hand over his chest and snuggled my cheek under his chin, listening to his heart beating. It was hammering fast, just like mine.

Good. I didn't want to be the only one in deep emotional trouble here. Logically, I knew he was mine. But experience told me that was most likely temporary. Men didn't seem to want to stick when it came to me.

But he wasn't a man, right? He was an alien. My *perfect* match.

Still, he didn't know me yet. We'd barely spoken a handful of sentences. What if I said something really stupid? He had already mentioned our age gap multiple times and said I was too young. I had no idea how old he was. I didn't care. He was sexy. Smoking hot.

Maybe I could just keep him in bed all the time. His body was rock hard. The unforgiving press of his weapons on the insides of my thighs had turned me on like I was some kind of freak. I loved that he'd fucked me with his pants still on, that deadly weapons had been rubbing the insides of my thighs. His fangs were long and sharp and so freaking hot that my core became wet again just thinking about it. Could he feel that? Was his cock sensitive enough to know I'd just flooded lust juice all over him?

Lust juice. That was a new one. My high school English teacher would be so proud. The thought made me smile. His hand stilled on my back where he'd been slowly, gently petting me. It didn't take much for him to caress my entire back. His palm covered nearly half. He was so much bigger than me. A grown man—alien—not a self-centered, narcissistic man-child who only wanted to use me to boost his career.

"What is funny, mate?"

"I was just thinking we should stay naked for the rest of our lives."

His soft chuckle made me all warm and tingly. "Did you not have a sufficient quantity of orgasms?" He shifted his hips just enough to make me gasp as his cock bumped the entrance to my womb.

"Is there a sufficient quantity?" I teased, already

feeling my skin flush, my nipples hardening into points against his chest.

"We shall find out."

I squealed in surprise as he lifted me in his arms and stood all in one smooth motion.

How freakishly strong was he?

He carried me to what I had recognized as the bathing room and turned on a stream of warm water. Placing me on my feet, he ordered me to move under the spray. I did, the heat welcome. I wet my hair as he leaned down and kicked off his boots, then pulled his pants off, leaving everything in a disorganized heap on the hard floor.

My jaw dropped. I couldn't help it. He was incredible. Thighs rippling with muscle, bigger than tree trunks. His chest and shoulders—already a huge fan—no longer looked out of place or freakishly huge. No, he was perfect. Massive chest, tapered waist, thighs that looked hard as diamonds, muscles layered over muscles and his cock...

Hard. Weeping with pre-cum. Ready to take me again.

I tore my attention away from his cock to find him watching me with an intensity that made my skin tingle.

"Do I pass inspection?"

I should have just said yes, but what fun was that? "Depends."

"What are your criteria?" His gaze narrowed as if he wasn't sure of my meaning, as if he were *unsure* whether I wanted him.

I lifted my hand and crooked one finger at him, beckoning him to join me under the water. He joined me immediately, my nipples pressed to his stomach as I craned my neck to look up into his eyes. Holding eye contact, I smiled as I wrapped both hands around his hard length. His sharp intake of breath was all the encouragement I needed.

"I need to be closer before I can say."

"I do not understand."

Moving slowly so I didn't startle him, I slid down onto my knees and took him into my mouth.

Two clenched fists pressed to the walls of the shower, but he held absolutely, perfectly still. I worked him gently at first, then hard, taking him deep and rubbing his balls until they swelled in a way I knew meant he was on the edge of coming.

Holding him in both hands, I popped his tip free and looked up into his face. I spent long seconds watching the water travel down his body in dark streams, washing the paint away from his chiseled face.

His skin nearly bare, I got my first real look at the face of my mate. He was gorgeous. Dark eyes, high cheekbones, a jawline that didn't quit. His hair was nothing more than a dark shadow on his head. He looked brutal. Intense. Like he could break me in half without trying. I knew he would never hurt me. Not if he was truly mine the way Warden Egara had promised. Being next to so much power and strength made me crazed with need. I wanted him pounding into my body, fucking me, biting me again.

I licked the tip of his cock like it was an ice cream cone. "This cock is mine."

His jaw clenched. His pulse pounded at his temples. "Yes."

"What do you think I should do with it?"

His body went rigid as if he were fighting himself.

"You're mine, Cormac. Tell me what you want."

With a shudder, he answered. "I want you to take me deep and swallow my cum down your throat. Then I'm going to fuck you up against the wall and bite you again so my mark is on both sides of your neck. So every fucking male who sees you will know you're mine."

"Hmmm." I ran my hand up and down his slippery cock, pretending to consider. There was no debate. "Up against the wall? In the shower?"

"Yes."

I licked him again and then held his gaze with the tip of his cock resting on my bottom lip. God, I was such a tease. Playing with fire, that's what I was doing. I knew it, and I couldn't stop. "Can you push me up against the wall and fuck me from behind?"

I ignored the rumble from his chest and ran my tongue up and down his length.

"Yes."

I loved the feeling of a man behind me, thrusting deep when all I could do was take what he chose to give me. Loved the way a cock rubbed me on the inside, hitting my sweet spot, making me crazy. I wanted Cormac's cock rubbing me just right. His heat at my back.

"Is that all you want?"

When he didn't answer, I looked up at him again and realized his knuckles were white, his jaw locked.

Playing with fire might have been an understatement. "Cormac?"

"No one has ever asked me."

"What you like during sex?"

He nodded slowly, and I stilled.

"Were you a virgin?"

"No. I have fucked many females."

"I don't understand." And I did *not* want to hear about his other women. A little green monster stirred inside me, and she was vicious, with really sharp teeth that poked holes in my confidence like a toothpick stabbing through a thin sheet of aluminum foil.

"The females are frightened by me. I am—" He looked away from me as he searched for words. "I—"

"You are what? Tell me."

He stared at the wall above my head. "I am often chosen to fuck. Never the same female twice."

How I could be angry that he hadn't had more lovers was beyond me, but I hurt for him as understanding dawned. He was just like me. Used for the thrill, for prestige, so the people he was with could brag about the conquest and their prowess. He was a high-ranking member of his legion. A hunter. A scary strong soldier of some kind. He'd told me he was a killer. I was a billionaire princess with millions of social media followers. The men I'd dated had been after status. Bragging rights. Fame.

Rage filled me at the hurt I knew he had buried deep. We'd both been used.

"You're mine now, Cormac. A thousand times won't be enough." To make my point, I took him deep, sucked hard and fast, pumping my mouth over him like a fist as I worked his balls with my hand. I scraped the fingernails of my other hand along the top of his thigh just hard enough to leave a mark.

He erupted in my mouth with a groan that sounded like agony, but I knew it was pure ecstasy. I took everything, swallowed him down, his heat making me feel powerful as he lost control, his hips pumping mindlessly.

When it was over, I lifted my mouth to the shower's spray and took several mouthfuls, rinsing him down, making sure nothing of his essence escaped. I was staking my claim. His body was mine. His cum was mine. His heart was going to be mine as well.

He watched me like a man possessed, like he couldn't look away. When I was finished, I stood slowly, dragging my nipples along his thighs, then his abdomen as I stood. I rubbed against him like a cat.

Without another word, he turned me around, lifted me with a hand around my waist and filled me from behind. The angle made him feel bigger. He stretched me, rubbing the sensitive spot inside my pussy with his length, making me pant and squirm.

He pumped into me in a relentless rhythm, and I

tilted my head to the side, exposing the unmarked side of my neck, the unbroken skin, in blatant invitation.

With a roar that made my pussy clench, his fangs sank deep. There was a spark of pain and then...bliss as whatever was in his bite filled me with heat. The orgasm built hard and fast, whatever he was putting into my bloodstream lighting up my clit like a firecracker.

I went off as he fucked me. Again a few moments later. Over and over until the cold wall and his arm were the only things keeping me upright. This time, when he came, he whispered my name against my skin and placed gentle kisses all over me as he rinsed us both off and carried me to bed.

He tucked me into his side under the covers. His heart beat under my ear. His heat enveloped me. He stroked over my back and hip in a soothing rhythm.

I went to sleep thinking this Interstellar Bride thing was pretty freaking perfect.

When I woke, everything fell apart.

6

Cormac

ying in the dark with my mate curled up next to me, trusting me to guard her, to give her what she needed, icy dread filled me, made my bones ache. I had never felt so vulnerable in my life. Abby was part of me now, a small, defenseless, desirable female who was mine to protect, to care for. I had no idea what a female might need outside the bedroom. None. The only female I spoke to regularly was Blade's sister, Silver, and she was an Enforcer as well. A killer like me. There was nothing soft about her.

Worse, there was no true safety for Abby here on the station. Styx security protected this room, but the alarms would only alert me to an attack, not help me defend this small, innocent female. My Abby. And she was mine.

Even now, my cock hardened at the thought of filling her again, waking her with a kiss, sliding into her wet heat. I wanted more.

I *needed* more. I couldn't go back to the solitary existence I'd had before. Didn't want to. I didn't want to keep fighting unless I had her to come home to.

The effects of my bite, my protection, were already showing. Her skin glowed with health. My scent marked every part of her as I was inside her now, in her blood, in her cells. My essence would keep her healthy, help her live longer, heal faster. She was mine. And I was alone out here. No one else from Styx legion was currently on the station, at least none I was aware of. If we'd had people here, I would have known. I didn't think to bring more fighters with me because I'd never needed them before. I hunted alone.

Hunting to kill and protecting someone else were two very different things.

Fuck.

I had to take her back to Rogue 5 immediately. There I would have the other Enforcers and mean as hell fighters to watch her back. To look out for her. To protect her. I wouldn't sleep easy until she was surrounded by my legion, in the heart of our territory where nothing and no one could reach her.

With slow, gentle movements, I untangled Abby's limbs from mine and slid out of bed. Releasing a sigh that made my chest ache, she nestled down into the covers and fell back into a deep sleep. I had exhausted my little mate and had plans to do so again and again, as often as possible. Before her, I'd been content to take my lovers as they came. But looking at the curve of her hip under the sheet, the soft swell of her breasts, I wanted to lay her on her back and feast on her pussy, lift her hips off the bed as I fucked her. I wanted to bite her, pump my seed and my essence into her as she whimpered and sobbed and her pussy spasmed all over my cock.

By the gods, I had to get a fucking grip.

Forcing myself to turn away from pure temptation, I used the S-Gen machine to make clean clothes for both of us. Mine, the usual uniform. Hers? I considered a soft, flowing gown the same blue as her eyes. No. One shot from an ion blaster and she would be dead.

Instead, I used the information in her transport data to create a fully functional set of very small armor, complete with Styx legion's specialized blast deflectors and the silver armband that would discourage most from bothering us. I also made her a helmet. I did not expect anything to go wrong, but her size—and the fact that she was with me—would attract enough attention without exposing her beautiful face and golden hair to the numerous scumbags I knew frequented the station.

One look and any idiot would know Abby was from Earth, and human females were widely sought after. Cerberus, the leader of another legion, had literally been killed in an ill-fated attempt to steal a human female for himself. No great loss; he had been cruel and without honor. His replacement, the new Cerberus, was a female named Jillela. She was a much better leader for their legion.

Unfortunately, he was not the only threat out there.

A quick comm to the repair bay and I was informed my ship would be ready to leave within the hour. Excellent.

I returned to the bedroom, fully dressed, armed to the teeth—I'd used the S-Gen to produce several additional weapons to protect my mate. I sat on the bed with my back pressed to the wall, alert, watching over Abby as she slept.

~

"I can't believe you're making me wear this." Abby's quiet complaint threatened to disturb the menacing glare I'd been holding in place from the moment we left our quarters. She walked next to me, covered head to toe in armor with a helmet on her head and the Styx legion's silver armband on display for all to see.

"This is a dangerous place. I explained this to you." I'd even given her a small ion blaster and shown her how to use it. She'd been naked at the time, which meant I'd been distracted by the need to spread her wide on the chair and lick her pussy until she begged me to take her.

I'd bitten her again, as well. I was out of control. Out. Of. Control. I'd spent less than a day in her presence, and my mate had somehow managed to completely destroy me.

We made it to the ship without incident, and I told Abby to wait at the entrance while I did a quick sweep. Once I knew the ship didn't have any unwelcome guests, I settled her in the co-pilot's seat and went back out to inspect the work I'd had done.

Modified thrusters and an upgrade to the power line that operated the onboard S-Gen machine. Most ships this small did not have one, but this was my brother's ship, the flagship for Styx legion, and we made sure it had the best equipment our credits could buy. What we couldn't buy, we stole. That was just our way.

Inspection done, I boarded the ship, locked us in and joined Abby. She had removed her helmet, her golden hair falling around her shoulders. She'd asked me if the S-Gen machine could produce something called a 'scrunchy' for her hair. My blank stare had made her shake her head and tell me to 'never mind.' When I'd asked what *that* meant, she told me to forget about it.

I did not ask more questions but vowed to ask Styx's human mate, Harper, about it later. If my mate wanted one of these 'scrunchy' things, she would have one.

"Are you strapped in?"

Abby patted the shoulder harness, the straps obviously too loose. "Yep."

Bending over her, I tightened the straps—*all of them* —despite her protest.

"That's too tight."

"No. That will keep you in your seat."

"Okay, grumpy pants. What's the matter with you? Did you wake up on the wrong side of the bed this morning?"

"What does the side of a bed have to do with my pants?" I buckled myself into the pilot's seat, my straps equally as tight. They had saved my life more than once.

"Nothing. But what's wrong? You seem to be in a very unhappy mood. Are you angry with me?"

"Absolutely not." The power core and propulsion systems fully operational, I steered us out of the station's docking bay as I considered what to tell her. I could not tell her the truth, that I had become consumed with worry, with the need to protect her. "The station is not safe for you. I simply want to get us home as quickly as possible."

Free of the docking bay, I accelerated the ship to move us clear of traffic. When she did not respond I glanced over to see her eyes wide and her knuckles white where her hands curled over the ends of the arms of her seat. "Are you unwell?"

"I'm—I've never been on a spaceship before." She glanced at the side monitor. "Is that a galaxy?"

"Yes."

"I've never seen this many stars." A tear gathered in her eye, swelled and then slid down her cheek. She wiped it away quickly.

"Why are you crying?"

"It's too much. It's just overwhelming and beautiful."

I glanced at the monitors and tried to see things through her eyes. Years ago, when I'd first left the safety of Rogue 5's star system, I'd been awestruck, as she was now. Countless stars in every direction, planets twinkling, the nearest galaxy a spiral of glowing pink and red. "I suppose it is." I pointed at a particularly bright star. Close. "That one is home." And to a pair of large, twinkling planets on the way. "Those two planets are Latiri 4 and Latiri 7. A lot of Coalition battles happen there. We will keep our distance, but they are going to be the only planets close enough to see until we get to Hyperion."

She tried to lean forward to inspect the planets on the monitor, but the seat's safety straps did their job. "I am not a fan. I can't move."

"That is their purpose."

"Seems like a bit much."

"Does it?" For the first time since I could remember something that felt like playfulness burst to life inside me. I grinned and accelerated.

"Ahhhhh!" Abby screamed, then laughed, the sound lighting a warm flame behind my ribs that I'd never felt before. I wanted more.

"That's worse than riding a rollercoaster."

"What is a rollercoaster?"

"It's a—well, it's a track. We strap ourselves into small seats and ride on the tracks. Sometimes there are huge drops and loops, and they go really fast."

"They sound terrible. Why would you do that?"

"For fun."

"Fun?"

"Yes. Fun, you old curmudgeon." She looked at me, and the sparkle in her eyes, the excited flush on her cheeks, made my cock hard. Gods, she was fucking beautiful. What the fuck was she doing with me? And what, exactly, was a curmudgeon? My IPU struggled to make sense of the word. Surely it did not mean what my language processor had implied?

"What is this word, curmudgeon?"

She lifted a brow, and I saw another new expression on her face, one I recognized all too easily from my time spent interacting with and observing my brother's human mate, Harper. Yes, I knew that look on a human woman's face. My little mate was about to cause me trouble.

"You know, cranky. Boring. Disagreeable. Doesn't like anything. Hates having fun."

My immediate reaction was to scowl and turn away, shame making my throat close and my head heavy. Did she believe me to be this way? I was unsure, as members of the legion rarely dared speak to me. None dared tease me if that was, indeed, what this female attempted.

Logically, what she stated about me was nothing but the truth.

"Cormac?"

"We will be traveling for some time. You should get some rest."

"Buckled in like this? No way. It's worse than trying to sleep on an airplane."

"It is the safest way."

My mate's silence communicated her misery clearly. I did not need to look at her to know she was coming to realize the bride processing protocols had made a terrible mistake. I was not fit to be mated to someone so innocent and full of hope. My mate should be hardened by life. Tough. A warrior like me. Then everything I did would not be such a disappointment.

"You big grumpy bear."

I looked up just in time to see my mate moving to straddle my lap. Once she was seated, I still needed to look down into her face, but not far. Not far at all. Her lips were close. Too close.

"I am not a bear."

"Oh, I think you are. A big."

She kissed me, a soft, slow, gentle kiss.

"Warm."

My cock, already hard as iron, ached as she kissed me again, this time on the tip of my nose. Then my cheek. My chin.

What the fuck was this female doing? I strained to lean forward and pull her tightly to me, but the restraints held me in place, as did my need to keep an eye on the ship's controls.

"Teddy bear."

I groaned as she trailed kisses along my jaw to my ear, then down the side of my neck. I felt like a fool, tilting my head to the side to give her better access, but she was conquering my will with nothing but two soft lips and the slight weight of her body on my lap.

"What is a teddy bear?"

Her lips hovered over my ear as she answered. "Something I like to cuddle with. Sleep with. Something that makes me feel safe and warm and protected."

"You will not sleep with this bear. You will sleep with no one but me." Rage filled my body with heat as the thought of her in another's bed formed in my mind. Since childhood, I had been cursed with a very vivid imagination. On the hunt, creativity was priceless. At the moment, that gift acted as a source of torment.

She laughed softly, and I turned to find her looking up at me with an expression I had rarely seen, the softness I had once witnessed passing between Harper and her second mate, Blade, when they thought no one was looking. I had never even hoped a female would look at me in such a way. "You want to keep me all to yourself?"

"Yes." Gods be damned, it was true. I didn't care if the processing had made a fucking mistake. I didn't care if I was cursed with a foul temper and a gift for killing our enemies. Who would keep her safe if not me? Who would protect her better than I?

No one. Fucking no one.

I was keeping her, and I didn't care if the gods tried to damn me for it. I'd already been cursed at birth. What else could they do to me?

"Come on." Abby kissed me one more time and crawled off my lap. "Does this thing have autopilot or whatever? Can it fly itself?"

"Yes, but I do not use that function so close to enemy territory."

"Hmmm." Abby ran the tip of her finger over my bottom lip. "How often do you fly through this area? Hundreds of times?"

"Thousands."

"And have you ever been attacked?"

"No. But there is always..."

My throat closed as Abby removed the armored shirt I had generated for her earlier. Her gaze held mine as she backed toward the exit that led to the rest of the ship. "How about we play a game?"

I barely managed to swallow around the lump in my throat. "What kind of game?"

"Hide and seek." She pulled the soft undershirt up and over her head as she stepped farther away from me, baring exposed skin. Small, round breasts. Nipples peaked from arousal? Excitement? Cold? I didn't know and I didn't care. I simply *wanted*.

"What are the rules?" Everything had rules. Everything.

"You close your eyes and count to twenty, out loud, while I hide."

"And then?"

"You find me."

"No." I glanced at the scans and data reports streaming into the ship's systems. Nothing of concern at the moment, but that could change at any...

She was gone. So were her clothes.

"Abby?"

Silence.

"Abigail! You will answer me! This is not safe!" I began unbuckling my flight harness. "Abby? Come back here!" Fuck. She could open the wrong panel. Trip and fall. Hit her head. Fall down a ladder and break her leg or her ankle. We could be attacked, and I would be forced to take evasive action, which would throw her around the ship like unsecured cargo. "Abby!"

Silence.

"Fuck. Fuck. Fuck." I set the controls to autopilot and set the alarms to sound through every level of the ship. Free of the harness, I stomped into the corridor and closed my eyes, allowed my ancient Everian Hunter blood to surge to life inside me like a wild thing. Normally, I equated this feeling with a need for battle. To hunt. Track. Kill.

Not this time.

I stumbled into the wall as the primal urge to find and claim my *mate* made my head spin. She had challenged me to a hunt, which I now realized was the most dangerous thing she could have done. I wasn't sure I could maintain control once I found her, not with the Hyperion savagery tearing at me to...take what was *mine*.

Several seconds passed as I gained a modicum of control, fought off the dizziness and the shock.

I stood, breathing in her scent, already searching for her as I did what she had asked and counted out to twenty in a loud voice.

I would find her.

I would strip her naked.

I would fuck her until she knew exactly who she belonged to, who she taunted.

My fangs dripped in anticipation.

7

Abby

*B*iting my lip to hold back a giggle—half glee, half fear—I watched through the ceiling's air duct panel as Cormac reached under a storage chest and found the panties I'd left there for him, smeared with wet goodness from my very aroused body.

His roar of frustration made my eardrums rattle, and I barely held back a full-blown laugh.

"I know you are in the ducts, female! Get out of there now!"

Nope. Not going to happen. He was too small to fit, and I had access to almost every room on the ship. I'd left my shirt in what was obviously a bedroom—and borrowed a very large t-shirt from a drawer so I didn't have to crawl through the ducts naked. My bra I abandoned in a storage room filled with big boxes strapped to the floor with harnesses that made the one I'd been wearing look like it was for a baby. I'd left one sock in a second smaller sleeping area with stacked beds that looked like crew quarters and the other in a room full of weapons.

I was headed toward the engine or power area now. The buzzing sound caused by whatever made this ship run was getting louder the farther I went.

Cormac growled. I didn't dare move as he lifted my pale purple panties to his nose and breathed deep.

My pussy clenched at his obvious pleasure. I dared a glance at his lower half and saw that his cock was rock hard and the bulge clearly visible beneath his black uniform pants.

God. He was going to ravish me.

Hell yeah. *He was going to* RAVISH *me.*

I didn't dare move until he left the room, probably in search of my pants—also perfumed with proof of my arousal—which I'd stashed in a room next door. The ship wasn't large, but it was just big enough for me to have some fun. Didn't hurt that I was sure this duct system and the steady stream of air gently blowing past me spread my scent through the entire ship. The fact that the ship was small no doubt helped make sure my smell was thick in every single room.

Moving quickly and quietly, I slid along the duct toward the buzzing sound. I was sure I would end up in some kind of ship operation room or somewhere full of control panels. Perfect place to leave a boot.

I made good time, wedged myself around a tight corner and stopped dead in my tracks. There was a weird box blocking my way. Ocean blue with half a dozen odd gadgets stacked across the top. I grinned as they looked like a line of little rubber ducks. The box itself filled half of the space, tucked neatly between the air duct's two walls, with the ducklings taking up another quarter of the height between floor and ceiling. I was small, but there was no way I was getting past that.

Damn it.

Wiggling my way back was a hell of a lot harder than crawling forward. The t-shirt I had on rode up past my thighs to bunch under my bare breasts.

Contortionist. I was adding it to my resume.

Once I made it around the corner and back into a straight area long enough for me to rest, I settled onto the cool material, breathing heavily. It wasn't metal, not like I'd seen in the movies. These ducts were smooth, and they shimmered like polished marble.

Weird.

"Abby."

Oh shit. His voice was close. Too close.

I stopped breathing, my heart rate going sky high as I held as still as a statue.

"Mate, I am coming for you."

Are you, Cormac? Can't find me, big bad alien?

I smiled. I hadn't had this much fun in years. Maybe ever.

The base of the duct collapsed beneath me. I cried out as I fell...

Straight into Cormac's arms.

"I win." Cormac's fierce expression had me clenching my thighs together. He was hot. So freaking sexy.

"Took you long enough." Silly me just had to bait the tiger.

Cormac's eyes darkened, and he lowered his nose to my bare belly, lower to the wet heat between my legs. With the t-shirt still bunched up over my ribs, all I had on downtown were my boots.

He took his time, breathing me in before moving back up my body. When he reached the shirt, he stopped.

"You have another male's scent on you."

"What?" He had to be talking about the shirt I'd borrowed. I had no idea who it belonged to, just that it was big enough to cover me up as I crawled around.

"Blade."

"Who's Blade?"

"Not your mate."

With none too gentle hands, he set me on my feet and pulled the shirt up over my head. Now *all* I had on were my boots. He took his time, inspecting every inch of my body. For what, I wasn't sure, but I'd never felt more alive. More beautiful. Sexier.

"You are unharmed?"

"I'm fine."

With a growl that brought goose bumps to my skin, he lifted me off the floor and turned me around to face the wall. Once there, he held me up with an arm around my waist as he freed his cock. Still holding me in place, he stepped between my legs. "I'm going to fuck you now, mate. Fuck you until you scream my name."

Well then, I was never going to scream. I was so wet, so swollen and achy and aroused by making him hunt for me that I nearly broke that vow the first time he pumped his hard cock into me from behind.

"Oh god."

"Your god cannot save you from me."

Great news because I didn't want to be saved. I needed to be taken. Craved. Desired. I wanted Cormac to put me first. My brittle heart dared hope he might actually fall in love with me.

My mate. Mine. For the first time since my mom died when I was a child, someone felt like they were mine.

I shifted my hips, opening myself up for him to go just a bit deeper.

We both groaned as he set a relentless pace with his enormous cock. He stretched me open and took what he wanted. Hard. Fast. An orgasm rolled through me, and I had to bite my upper arm to stop the scream from escaping my throat because I was afraid he would keep his word. Afraid he would stop if I screamed.

The bite hurt just enough. I gasped as the pain sent my nerves into overload and intensified my release. I was out of my head. Nothing existed but Cormac and his cock and the wall holding me in place so he could take more.

His cock swelled, and he bottomed out inside me and stopped moving. "Not yet, mate." His fangs grazed the curve of my neck, my shoulder, and I shuddered in anticipation.

"Do it."

"Do what?"

"Bite me."

"Not yet. You will wait." He stepped back, carrying me with him, his arm like a steel band around my waist.

I didn't really care what he did, as long as he kept giving me orgasms.

He carried me down the corridor with my back to his chest, cock buried deep, my hands locked onto his forearm and my legs wrapped around his thighs. He still wore all of his clothing, all of it. I was naked except for my boots. I tried to imagine the picture we made and shivered at the vision in my mind. So erotic. Exotic. So not me. Not until him.

Cormac pulled free and laid me down on the large bed in the center of the room where I'd helped myself to a shirt.

I whimpered when his cock left my body. I sobbed when he rolled me onto my back and his lips locked onto my clit. He sucked the sensitive nub into his mouth. He wasn't shy like the human men I'd been with. He devoured me like I was his favorite treat. Lips. Tongue.

Two fingers moving in and out of my swollen core. My back arched off the bed. I was on the edge.

He stopped, and I looked down to find him staring at me, his fangs clearly visible, a drop of liquid coating his lower lip.

The sight had me licking mine. I wanted that drop. I wanted him to bite me *down there.*

"Yes. Yes. Yes. Yes." The word became a chant as he lowered his mouth to my pussy once more, filled me with his tongue, moved higher. His tongue worked my clit as his fangs settled in the soft mound of flesh just above. I lifted my hips off the bed, trying to force him to hurry the hell up.

Fangs sank deep. My clit exploded as the essence of my mate flooded me *down there.* My pussy spasmed stronger than a pulsing heart, each beat making me thrash on the bed as he pushed his fingers deep.

I screamed. His name? I had no idea. I was blissed out, basically having an out-of-body experience.

The bite went on and on, the heat of his claim spreading to every part of me from fingertips to toes. I felt drunk on pleasure. Stoned. Except this was better than any drug I'd ever tried. Way better than alcohol.

"Cormac." I reached for him, wanting to pull him toward me, but there was nothing to grab onto except...him.

Luckily, I didn't have to say more. He withdrew his fangs and kissed the spot before standing over me like a sex god. He undressed quickly before crawling up the bed toward me.

His lips found mine, and I locked my arms around his head. The heat of his skin pressed down, and I was in heaven. I never wanted to let go. Never wanted this to end. "I think I'm falling in love with you."

He froze like I'd slapped him. Did he not want me to say that? Did that freak him out? He was my mate, right? Like, he was stuck with me? He would fall in love with me. He had to. That was what I was promised by Warden Egara. A man, alien, perfect for me.

"I'm sorry. I shouldn't have said that."

"It is not possible. Not yet." The denial broke his trance, and his lips found mine with long, exploratory kisses that made my heart ache. Yep, I was in trouble here.

Why did he say that? Did he think his own mate wouldn't love him? I could relate, but he was freaking amazing. Why would he think that? Why had he gone silent and stone-faced when I said the "L" word?

Stupid. I never learned to keep my mouth shut. I always just said what I was feeling. That habit had always gotten me into trouble. Apparently, I hadn't learned my lesson.

His kisses were like a drug. I locked my legs around his thighs and tugged at him to move his cock where I knew we both ached for him to go.

We were both silent as he slid deep. He took his time,

slowly increasing the rhythm of his thrusts until I couldn't take anymore. I cried out as another release blasted through me, amplified by the essence of his bite still circulating in my body, in my blood. By him. His heat. His strength. The smell of his skin. I was addicted, and I would never get enough.

He covered me, his heavy weight like a blanket as he filled me with his seed. I'd told Warden Egara I wasn't ready for kids—and taken suitable precautions. That didn't stop me from imagining my big, scary teddy bear with toddlers crawling all over him like he was a jungle gym. He wouldn't forget about our children, ignore them or leave them behind. He wouldn't treat them like they were invisible.

He wouldn't ever treat *me* like I was invisible, either. Even now, he held himself up with his elbows on either side of my head so I could breathe. He shuddered as the aftereffects of his own orgasm continued to ride him. I ran my fingernails gently up and down his sides, everywhere I could reach, petting him, letting him know he mattered to me.

He kissed me one more time before lifting his head to glare down at me. Which was a bit humorous with his cock still buried deep. That, and he couldn't stop looking at my lips.

"Abby, what were you doing crawling around in the ventilation system? That was not a good idea."

"I thought it was an excellent idea."

He rocked his hips, his cock shifting inside me until I

was on the verge of asking him to start all over again. Hell, I was going to be sore, and I didn't care.

"I couldn't reach you. What if you'd been trapped in there? I will not have you place yourself in danger."

"I was fine." I lifted my head and kissed his shoulder, nipping at him just a little. His hips jerked in response, so I did it again. "If it weren't for that stupid rubber duck box blocking me, I would have made it to another room and left a boot for you." I lifted my leg as much as I could to make my booted foot visible from the corner of his eye. "But I'm glad I didn't. Boots have excellent traction."

With a chuckle, he rolled to the side and pulled me with him. His hard length slipped free, and I sighed at the loss. I loved the feel of him inside me. I felt like we were one, like I really belonged. Like I mattered to him.

"I have never used autopilot on a ship. Not once."

"What if the flight is really long? Don't you need to sleep?"

"I can go several days without sleep before I become compromised. Generally, it does not take that long to get where I need to go."

"Several days?" I rested my head on his shoulder, content when his arm settled behind me, holding me against him.

"Yes."

He held me. He was big. Warm. Safe.

I never wanted to move again.

8

Cormac

uck me. I'd been so distracted by my mate —and my out-of-control instinct to claim her—that I'd ignored her statement.

If it weren't for that stupid rubber duck box blocking me, I would have made it to another room...

I yanked my uniform back on as quickly as I could manage while being distracted watching my clean, naked mate put on the fresh set of clothing I'd generated for her after our shower. I'd been obsessed with bathing her, couldn't tolerate the smell of Blade on her skin. I'd washed her with my own hands, fucked her slowly in the shower, generated some food and delighted in watching her consume something called lasagna like it was the most delicious thing she'd ever tasted. I tried a bite but did not care for the acidic taste of the red paste.

I'd pounded down several nutrition bars and some fluid designed for my Hyperion system and then stared at her as she moved food to her mouth. Chewed. I'd watched the flow of her neck muscles as she swallowed and allowed my gaze to wander down to her curved breasts. Watching a naked female eat was one of the most erotic things I'd ever seen. My fangs had dropped. I wanted to bite her again. And again.

I'd lost my damn mind. How someone so small could wield so much power over me was a mystery I might never unravel. All I knew was every time I looked at her, I *wanted.*

And now that obsession had put her in danger. There were no boxes in the ventilation system. I knew because they were purposely left empty so we could smuggle goods in the tight space. Styx legion had specially designed containers that hooked together in a chain for easy removal once we reached our destination. They were also designed to look exactly like the rest of the space. An inspector could like right at them and see nothing.

Definitely not a rubber duck box, whatever the fuck that was.

None of our smuggling containers blocked more than half of the space. Abby would have been able to pass by one of ours. It would be a tight squeeze for her, but she could have done it. She was so damn small. Vulnerable. Weak. How was I going to protect her?

Impatient now, I watched as Abby finished putting on her boots. She looked her part once more, wearing the Styx legion's armored uniform with the silver band on her arm. And I could breathe knowing she had at least some protection.

"Come." I held out my hand, half afraid she would refuse to take it after the way I'd fucked her earlier. I'd been out of control. Completely feral.

I nearly sighed with relief when her soft hand slid into mine and she smiled up at me. "Where are we going?"

"Back to pilot controls. I need to scan the ventilation system." I took a step but encountered resistance. Abby had her heels dug into the floor and was trying to pull me back to her. "You are not strong enough to move me."

"I don't want to move you. I want *you* to kiss *me*. Then I'll go with you."

"This is not a game, Abigail."

"Oh, I know, mate. This is our life. Much more important."

I considered her words. She was mine, my female, my mate. I wanted her to be happy, to choose to be with me. And I wanted to kiss her at least as much as she wanted the kiss.

Instead of moving to her, I tugged her to me and gently took her lips with mine. I buried my fingers in her damp hair and groaned as the soft scent of her surrounded me once more. When my cock rose to attention, I pulled back. "That is enough. I do not have time to fuck you properly."

Her laughter was a cool breeze blowing through the hell I'd lived in most of my life. "You already did that. More than once."

"Not enough."

She smiled, her hand resting on my cheek. "It's probably a good thing. I'm not used to so much activity, and I'm pretty sore."

"You do not feel well?"

"I feel great. I'm just a little sore. You know, down there."

"Unacceptable." Lifting her in my arms, I cradled her to my chest and carried her to the co-pilot's seat. While she buckled in, I removed a ReGen wand from a storage cabinet and placed the glowing green wand between her legs, right up against her pussy.

"What?" She looked down at the healing device, then back up at me, a drunken look coming over her. "Oh. That's nice. I gotta get me one of these."

"We have dozens of them at home." Home. With her. I liked the sound of that.

"Really?"

"I do not lie."

Now that my mate was properly taken care of, I returned my attention to the control panel and began running scans on the ventilation system. Saw nothing. Ran the scans again. Still nothing.

"Where did you see this rubber duck box?"

She had her head tilted back, and her eyes closed when she answered. "Right around the corner from where you made me fall from the ceiling." She opened her eye and peered at me through the corner of the nearest one. "Which you wouldn't have been able to do if that stupid box hadn't been in my way."

I glanced down at the ReGen wand, saw that the device's lights indicated it had finished healing my mate. I held out my hand, palm up. "All better?"

"Yes. Thank you." Abby placed the wand in my hand, and I was intrigued to see her cheeks turn a shade of pink.

"Why are you turning pink?"

"What?" She turned to face away from me. "I'm not."

"Are you unwell?" I left my seat to kneel next to her, running the ReGen wand over her from head to toe.

"Stop that. I'm fine."

"Then why are you changing color?"

She grabbed my wrist to stop the scan, her small fingers unable to completely wrap around me. "It's called a blush. It happens when I'm embarrassed. It's no big deal. I'm fine."

"Then show me this box."

"You won't be able to fit in there. It's a tight squeeze."

"That is why you will carry this." I returned the ReGen wand to its compartment and removed an advanced comm device with video broadcast capabilities. The comm was small, meant to be hidden during missions where Styx wanted evidence or proof of someone's deeds. Abby would not have difficulty taking it along. "You will carry this, and I will monitor you from here. I will see what you see."

"Okay." She unbuckled and reached for the comm. I lifted it out of reach and looked down into her eyes. "You are not to touch the box, do you understand? I do not know what it is, and it may be dangerous."

"Okay. Point this thing at it. Don't touch it. Got it."

Fifteen minutes later, I watched on the monitors as Abby approached the box from the propulsion station's side. She'd already crawled down the vent to where she'd first seen the box. I could not ascertain its nature from that angle, nor was it responding well to standard scans.

I'd taken her to the next duct panel in the line and asked her to crawl back through it so I could see the opposite side of the object.

What I'd seen had made my heart stick in my chest, my blood suddenly so thick it felt like glue trying to slog its way through my system.

Siren's symbol. My legion's enemy. My brother's enemy. My enemy.

"Abby, get out of there now."

"What? What's wrong?"

"Get out of there. Do not touch it. I am coming." I ran to the open panel just as Abby's feet appeared. She kept moving backward, her feet lowering into the room, followed by her legs, her thighs, that luscious, round ass.

Not wanting to wait, I reached up and lifted her the

rest of the way down. Once she was safely back in my arms, I crushed her to me for a few seconds.

"What's wrong?"

"That symbol on the side is from the Siren legion. They are dangerous enemies."

"Well, that's not good."

"No. The swirling red lights are a timer, and it is counting down. I have been unable to scan the contents, but we must assume it is an explosive device."

"Oh, shit." She pulled back and looked up into my face, alarm clear in her wide eyes and her dilated pupils. "How long? Will it destroy the whole ship? Can you turn it off? Or shoot it out into space?"

"If my calculations are correct, it is set to detonate about two hours after our arrival on Rogue 5."

"What? I don't understand. Rogue 5 is still hours away."

"They are trying to use me to destroy my brother, the leader of our legion. This is his personal ship. After our arrival, it will not go into the public docking bay but deep inside Styx territory. Many of our people would have died had we not played your game, had the Siren device remained hidden."

"So, what are we going to do?"

"You are going to come with me and buckle into your seat. I am going to stop this ship and contact Styx for instructions. Most likely he will send a team to evacuate us."

"Why not keep going? If we meet them halfway, it will be faster."

We covered the short distance to the control room and buckled into our seats. "Some of these devices have proximity sensors. I can't assume the target is my brother. I have many enemies. Should someone wish to kill me, the explosive could be triggered by the protections and scanners we have in place on the edge of our space. Or it could be programmed to detonate in a specific area of space."

"What about a remote control?"

I shook my head. "No. The lining of our ships is specially designed to block all communication and signals that do not come in through the ship's designated sensors."

"So...if you're smuggling something, no one can figure out what you have on your ship?"

"Exactly." I found myself smiling. "We will make a pirate of you yet."

"I don't know about that. But whoever it is better not be trying to kill you. I'll have to hunt them down and—"

"And?"

"I don't know. But I'd do something. I may be small, but I can be sneaky."

I glanced over at my mate to find her completely serious. Fierce. A small creature spitting fire to protect me. *Me.*

Absurd. No one protected me. I was the monster, the

Enforcer. A killer. I was Styx's right hand and his executioner. I was the hunter, not the prey.

So why did her words make me feel like I would kneel at this female's feet? Do anything to make her happy? To protect her? To make fucking certain she never had to face off with anyone, especially not one of Siren legion's thugs?

Fuck. She owned me, and she didn't even know it.

Watching the monitor I'd instructed Abby to leave in place near the explosive device, I slowed the ship, then brought us to a halt. I commed the nearest relay that would give me access to Rogue 5 and waited impatiently for my brother to answer. He'd better fucking answer. I used our private emergency codes.

Seconds later, the comm screen lit up with Styx's very annoyed face. "This better be good, brother." Styx was naked, his tattoos clearly visible from the chest up on the screen. He looked like he'd just left Harper in bed.

"It is."

Behind him, a female's cries of pleasure rang out loud and clear. Abby put her hand over her face, covering her eyes as if she didn't dare look. Her cheeks had that same pink blush I'd questioned her about earlier.

"Tell Blade to stop. Harper's cries are upsetting my mate."

Styx shook his head. "You tell him to stop giving his essence to our mate. I dare you."

Fuck. Not touching that one. The bite we gave our mate was sacred.

I looked over at Abby. "Are you all right?"

"I'm fine." The words were quiet, as was the laughter I realized she hid behind her hands.

"Cormac. Why aren't you home? And what the fuck do you need? I'm a little busy here."

"My apologies, brother. I am nearly halfway there. Sending our coordinates now."

"And?"

"Abby discovered a Siren explosive device onboard the ship. It has Siren legion's mark on the outside casing. I don't know if it is theirs or if someone just wanted us to think Siren attacked us. I cannot disable it. I tried. I need you to send Dax to take it apart, and I need a team out here to evacuate us."

"Fuck."

"I can't bring the ship in. The timer is set to go off soon after I would have been docked. It would have killed a lot of our people."

"Proximity trigger?"

"I don't know. I can't get a reading on it. The device is impervious to my scans."

"Fuck and fuck." Styx ran his hand over his chest, then settled it along the back of his neck. "Dax (DAXOR-DANIS – explosive specialist for Styx) will be on his way in ten minutes with a full evac team. Please tell your mate that I owe her a favor and that is a promise I don't make lightly. Don't do anything to set the damn thing off. I'm going to be really fucking furious if you get yourself killed."

The monitor went dark, and I turned as Abby burst into laughter. "Oh my god, how embarrassing. Is that what I sound like when you bite me?"

Not wanting to lie, I decided the truth was my only option. "No. Your cries have a higher pitch, and they make my cock hard as a rock."

"Cormac! You weren't actually supposed to answer that." Abby's hand covered her mouth, and she was hiding another fit of laughter.

"I told you, mate, I do not lie." I could not look away from the sparkle in her eyes and the happiness I saw there. I had never been the one to make someone else laugh. I found I enjoyed the feeling immensely.

Abby held my gaze for a moment before her hand dropped to her lap, and she scowled at something behind me. "Cormac. What is the bomb doing?"

9

Cormac

I turned around to look at the image on the screen. The timer light had changed color from red to blue. "Fuck. Get out of your seat. Now!"

"What? Why? What's happening?" Abby asked questions even as she worked to release herself from the harness holding her to the co-pilot seat. "Cormac?"

Out of my seat, I knelt next to Abby and assisted her with the last two buckles. Pulling her to her feet, I hit the comm button that would send a distress code to my brother. I didn't have time to wait for him to answer. I yelled into the air as I ran, pulling Abby behind me.

"Styx, this is Cormac. The device activated when the ship stopped. I am taking my mate to an escape pod. Find us!"

"Escape pod?" Abby's much shorter legs could not produce the speed required to get us off this ship alive. Turning, I picked her up and ran.

The ship had two pods, each capable of holding up to five people, nestled beneath the main body of the ship. When we reached the activation switch, I set Abby on her feet and placed my hand over the scanner. The hatch opened. I ignored the ladder and jumped down into the pod. Turning around, I held out my arms to my mate. "Jump!"

"That's like ten feet."

"Jump, female. Now!"

"Shit." Abby stepped off the edge above, and I caught her. Before she could ask any more questions, I set her on her feet and closed the hatch. The inside of the pod was hexagonal, with reinforced beams on either side of each personal protection bay. Under our feet was a small storage area with at least a week's worth of rations, environmental suits and some basic equipment.

I picked her up and placed her inside one. By my calculations, we had less than a minute to get the fuck off this ship.

Abby watched me as I buckled her into the harness. When I was done, I stepped into the pod opposite her and repeated the process on myself, thankful for the drills I'd had to complete during pilot training.

Half strapped, I gave the verbal command for the pod to launch.

Abby screamed as the pod was forcefully ejected from the ship.

"Are you unharmed?"

Abby looked at me, the pulse at the base of her neck pounding. "Yes. What now?"

"Now we—"

The loud roar of an explosion came through the escape pod's comm system. Abby jumped. I winced. Styx was going to be really fucking angry that someone had blown up his favorite ship.

"Was that?"

"Yes."

"God, that was close. We barely made it."

"Yes."

"Thank you. For carrying me. I was trying to keep up, but—"

"Mate, I will always protect you. You are mine."

Abby's eyes glittered, and I realized the effect was caused by gathering tears. She blinked, and two drops slid down her perfect cheeks. "Okay. As long as you're mine, too."

I held her gaze so she would know I meant what I said. "I am yours."

"Okay. Good." She wiped the tears from her face and took a deep breath. "What's going to happen to us now?"

I looked to my left, where one of the five control panels was located at shoulder level. The pods were built for Styx warriors, which explained why Abby's control panel was located over her head. She would not be able to see the controls to activate them.

Not acceptable. I would update Styx on this design flaw. What if he, Blade and his human mate, Harper, were here? The controls would be out of reach for his mate as well. What if Styx and Blade were injured and unable to function? No, this would not do at all.

I studied the data on my panel and frowned. "The pod will take us to the nearest known outpost or habitable planet. In this case, it is Latiri 4, a planet that has seen many Coalition-Hive battles."

"So we are landing in a war zone?"

"I don't know. Things have been quiet there for a few weeks, but I am not part of the Coalition. I do not know what kind of Hive activity is in the area. That would be Commander Karter's problem."

"Who's he?"

"He is the Prillon Commander of the closest Coalition Battle group. Karter is a warrior with honor. His warriors monitor this sector of space." I grinned as I remembered something that might ease my mate's fears. "His mate is a human female as well."

"Really?"

"Yes."

"Can I meet her?"

"No."

"What? Why not?" Her fear was gone, replaced with the defiance and fire I much preferred.

"I am an outlaw, mate. A criminal and a smuggler. We do not visit Coalition battleships for entertainment."

~

A bby

W ell, that sucked. One of the few human women out in space, and I wouldn't get to meet her because my mate happened to be a bad guy. "Will they kill you or something?"

"I don't believe so. Styx is normally the one to deal with any Coalition contact."

"But will this Commander Karter know you're a spy or whatever?"

Cormac finally turned away from the blinking panel near his shoulder and looked at me. "I am not a spy."

"Then what are you? What did you do to earn an Interstellar Bride? Warden Egara said you had to have helped the Coalition with something."

His yellow eyes darkened to a deep gold, and I immediately remembered this man was an alien. He didn't play by human rules. Probably didn't give two shits about what I thought was right or wrong. He had his own code. Sure would be nice to know what rules he *did* follow.

"We are smugglers, mate, but we are not without honor. The leader of our legion, Styx, is also my adopted brother. As a general rule, we do not interfere with the business of other legions unless provoked. However, we do support the Coalition's fight against the Hive."

"I don't understand."

"We are Styx. We honor family. Loyalty. And we take care of those weaker than ourselves. As an Enforcer, that is part of my job. I hunt those who prey on the weak, those who threaten our legion, those who disobey Styx, and those who think they are above our laws."

"And you kill them?"

"Yes." There was no apology in his tone. No shame. He simply stared at me and waited for me to accept or reject him.

"Is that— Is that your only job?"

"I provide our legion with information and advise my brother if asked. Otherwise, yes, that is my only job."

Whoa. I wasn't sure how I felt about his work, but I *was* sure how I felt about him. Hot. God help me, he was sex on a stick. "I want to kiss you right now."

His shoulders dropped slightly, and I realized he'd been tense, maybe expecting me to hate him now. Or be afraid?

Styx crossed his arms over his chest and glared down at me. "Any more questions?"

Why not bait the tiger? "You still didn't answer me. What did you do to earn a bride?"

"Coalition spies occasionally ask for our help smuggling illegal Hive technology, weapons, or prisoners. Sometimes they have an issue to deal with that would cause them political problems if they interfered directly. They appreciate our discretion."

"Is that all you are going to tell me?"

"Yes. To tell you more would put you at risk. You do not need to know."

Well, shit. Curiosity killed the cat and all that. "Okay."

Cormac's dark brow raised in disbelief. "You are satisfied?"

"No." I reached toward him, struggling to touch him. Thankfully, he lifted his much longer arm and laced his fingers with mine. Everything in me settled with that one simple touch. "I am curious as hell. But I trust you. You're one of the good ones."

"I am a killer."

Why was he arguing with me? "Yeah. That's what you said." Something blasted outside the pod, under my feet. It felt like we were on the inside of a rocket that had those thruster things I'd seen in the occasional science fiction movie. I wasn't really a fan, but two of my old boyfriends had been obsessed with every alien invasion and monster movie they could get their hands on.

Hah! Look who was actually in outer space now, bitches.

"Abby?"

I found my feet, thankful for the harness that had held me in place, and looked up at him. "What?"

"I do not believe you understand what I am."

My turn to raise an eyebrow. "You kill people who fuck with your family. I'm okay with that. Somebody has to do it. It's not like you have police or the FBI or anything like that." I frowned. "Or do you? Have police?"

"I am responsible for dispensing justice for my people."

"Styx decides, and you are his number one guy. I'm guessing he trusts you the most since you're his brother."

"Do you want to know how many people I have killed?"

"It doesn't matter to me." Shocked at how true that statement was, I leaned my head back against the wall behind me as nausea grabbed hold of my stomach with iron claws. Traveling in an escape pod sucked. I spoke through gritted teeth, hoping that if I didn't open my mouth, no vomit could come out of it. "Unless you want to tell me. Do you want me to know?"

"It is my burden to carry."

"You're afraid if I know the number, I won't love you anymore?"

Silence. He stared at me like I'd grown a second head.

Oh, shit. I'd just told him I loved him. Well, damn it, I did. Stupid? Probably. I'd always been one to give my heart away too fast and pay the consequences. I'd had countless people tell me to stop it. To wait. To not get too attached too quickly. You might as well tell my heart to stop beating. I was who I was. All I could do was hope this time I wouldn't get my heart broken.

The pod rattled and shuddered like a giant infant was shaking his favorite rattle. I closed my eyes and hoped like hell the pod wouldn't fall apart before we landed wherever we were going.

A loud roar filled the small space while I counted to thirty-two and then...hissing. Like gases coming out of a valve. Nothing moved. No rattling or roaring or shuddering.

"Did we land?" I opened my eyes to find Cormac still staring at me with an odd expression on his face.

"You are too young for me."

I rolled my eyes as I worked to unbuckle my harness. "Not this again. Tell me the number."

"I am several decades older than you."

"Don't care. The number, Cormac. It's not going to change the way I feel about you, so just tell me."

"You said you loved me."

"I do."

"That's impossible."

"Shut the hell up and tell me the number."

10

Abby

"One hundred and seventy-three outsiders. Three traitors inside the legion."

"One-seven-six. Got it." I released the last buckle and stepped away from the wall. "Are we on that planet? Ma-tear-ee? Whatever you said?" I might have paid more attention if I hadn't been so worried about dying when he told me.

"Latiri 4. Yes." Cormac unbuckled as well and turned to look at his control panel. "We are just outside an abandoned structure. We should be able to reach it easily. Perhaps a ten-minute walk."

"My legs are short. Better make that fifteen. Does this place have air we can breathe?"

"Yes, but it is not ideal. We will suit up, walk to the

base and take refuge inside until the evacuation team arrives."

"How will they know where we are?"

Cormac pointed to one of the flashing lights on his panel. "This beacon is coded for Styx legion only. Anyone else will only be aware of random light frequencies moving through space."

"A secret code. Cool." I looked around, ready to get the hell out of this pod. I wasn't claustrophobic, but this experience might change that. I wanted *OUT*. "Where are the suits?"

Cormac opened a panel on the floor and sorted through items. He placed a dark gray suit and helmet at my feet and removed a second for himself. The suits were accented with startling silver accents across the chest and a large band of silver on both upper arms. The helmet bore a brighter striping pattern as well. He lifted a large pack from below the floor as well. "These suits will filter and optimize the atmosphere so we can breathe it for days without any issue as well as protect us from radiation. The pack is full of rations and water."

He stood and opened another panel, this one at the back of the cubby I'd just been standing in. Inside were weapons. Space guns. Little silver pistols that looked like shiny toys. Big knives with blades that were black, not silver metal. They looked incredibly sharp.

Cormac removed everything. Every single weapon. I had no idea where he was going to put it all.

"Take off your clothes and put on the suit."

"Naked?"

"Yes." He was all business, not a hint of the passionate lover I'd been spending time with. This version of Cormac was intense. Abrupt. He made me feel like he had everything under control, but I also felt alone. Unseen. I realized terror was the spice running through my blood. I'd been riding an adrenaline rush, and now my hands shook so badly I couldn't get my clothes off.

"Cormac?"

"Yes?" He stuffed two knives and the weapons into the pack, leaving two small silver pistols and one larger, rifle-sized space gun on the floor. He had already set two knives on top of his suit.

I tried to answer, but it felt like my lungs were shaking. Impossible, but I couldn't keep my airflow steady.

Cormac stopped what he was doing and looked up at me. "Abby." His tone softened when he said my name. He stood, and I rushed into his arms. "You're shaking."

"I'm sorry. I think it's adrenaline."

With a gentleness I'd come to expect from him, he cupped the side of my face and lowered his head for a slow, dominant kiss. I relaxed into him with muscle memory I didn't realize I had. He was mine. He was safe. He was sexy. He was everything.

He pulled back and rested his forehead against mine. "Better?"

"Yes." I sighed. It wasn't from the kiss but from the strong feel of his arms around me. "But I'm still shaking."

I let him go and managed to strip and step into the

suit with bare feet. Built-in boots enveloped my feet, adjusting to fit perfectly. I pulled the suit up over my hips, got my arms in the correct holes and stopped cold at the sight of Cormac in his suit.

He was huge, I knew, but the suit hugged every curve, every muscle like a second skin. When he flexed, when he moved at all, I had to stop myself from staring. When I didn't move for several seconds, he turned his attention to me.

"That is the smallest suit we have. It was designed for Harper. Does it fit?"

"I don't know. I don't know how to zip it up."

"Zip it up?" He moved to stand in front of me, and I placed my palms flat on his chest. Mine. Mine. Mine.

"You know? Close it?"

"Indeed." He stepped toward me and slid his hand inside the suit, cupping my breast. I bit back a groan as he ran a rough thumb over my stiff nipple. "A shame to cover such beauty."

"Kiss me again."

He did, this time with a bit more urgency. When he stepped back, I swayed. He grinned and removed his hand from my body. I missed him at once.

"We should move. I don't believe anyone would have been able to track the pod, but I won't take chances with your life." He magically closed the front of my suit, the entire thing adjusting to my body like a living thing, hugging me everywhere. Cormac stepped back and admired the view for several seconds. I took the opportunity to do the same. "You are beautiful, mate."

"So are you."

Suddenly serious, he lifted one of the toy-sized pistols and held it out to me in one hand. The other held one of the black knives. "Have you ever fired a weapon?"

"Yes. I was practically raised by my father's security team. I can hit the bullseye almost every time from a hundred yards."

"I do not understand this distance."

I thought about a way to explain it to him. "If you ran as fast as you could for a count of ten and stopped, I'd be able to hit you between the eyes." I knew that was Olympic athlete speed for a hundred-meter sprint, but I'd seen Cormac run. He was *fast*.

"Close combat?"

"I'm even better."

"Excellent." He quickly went over the basic features of the weapon and showed me where to place the ion blaster in a specially made holster on the suit. "The blade goes here." He slipped the long knife into a pocket on the side of my thigh. The knife, and the pocket into which he'd placed it, disappeared. "If you need the blade, place your hand over the pocket, and the suit will respond. Otherwise, the weapon will remain hidden."

"Handy."

"Yes. It has saved my life more than once."

I lifted my hand to his face and ran my thumb over his lower lip. "Then I love it even more."

"Behave, mate."

"Not going to happen." I slipped the helmet he handed me over my head to the sound of his quiet laughter. I found it was a sound I very much enjoyed and vowed to make sure I could hear it more often.

He lifted the pack and secured it on his back. Helmet on, he took two steps and placed his hand on the wall. A doorway slid open. He walked out as if stepping onto an alien world was an everyday occurrence.

Heart racing with excitement, fear and a bunch of chaotic emotions I couldn't begin to sort through, I took my first step on a new world.

ormac

I was supposed to be scanning for danger, not watching my new mate's round ass swaying back and forth in front of me. We had just been forced to abandon ship, narrowly escaped death, and all I could think about was spreading the globes of her bottom wide and filling her pussy from behind. Or her ass. Maybe she'd allow that if I seduced her properly.

The more I thought about it, the more uncomfortable my suit became pressed against my hard cock.

I had to get my mind right. I would never touch her again if we were both killed on this fucked up rock. The battles that had taken place here between the Coalition Fleet and Hive forces were legendary, and I had no intention of being caught in the middle of the next one. And there would be another battle. And another. For some reason, the Hive seemed particularly interested in this sector of space. I didn't fool myself into thinking it had anything to do with Rogue 5 or our people. There was something else here. Something neither my legion nor the Coalition had figured out yet.

"How far do we have to go?" Abby's grumbled question snapped me to attention.

"Not much farther."

"How many steps? Because this measurement thing on my helmet display means nothing to me. I don't know what these abbreviations mean. I need meters. Or feet. Or miles. Something."

"Are you tired?"

She sighed. "I thought I'd be okay, but I think I'm having an adrenaline crash."

Not familiar with the human term, I closed the distance. I lifted my female into my arms and cradled her to my chest. Her head fell to my shoulder at once.

"I can walk."

"I am sure you are able. But you will not."

"I'll make your arms hurt."

I nearly burst into laughter at the thought that her slight weight would have any effect on me. "No, you will not. I could carry you this way for days, mate. You will not walk."

"Bossy." Her body relaxed in my arms. The complete trust made my chest fill as if it were about to burst from internal pressure. "But I like it."

"I will always take care of you, mate."

Abby was quiet for long minutes. I barely heard her whisper through my helmet comm.

"I'm beginning to believe you."

Now that my female was close to me and I was no longer distracted by watching her seductive movements, I covered the distance to the outpost the escape pod had identified as our best chance of survival. When I established line of sight, I adjusted my helmet scans to provide me with a close-up view of the structure.

It was old. Perhaps decades or more. And from the looks of it, abandoned. Broken-down equipment littered the ground outside of the building. The builders had placed the outpost directly into the side of a mountain of rock so only the front and main entrance were visible. The doors and walls remained intact. It was a fucking miracle our escape pod had discovered it.

Only the Hive must have left in a hurry. The Coalition was greedier with their materials. The Prillons and their Fleet would have torn down the walls, broken down and recycled the equipment, taken everything until there was nothing more to find than a bare rock. They absolutely would not have left any tech behind that might give their enemy an advantage. This place, however, looked like a trash heap with random items scattered everywhere.

Normally, I would rush the entrance and take whatever came my way. Just because the place looked abandoned didn't mean it truly was. But I had a mate now. I could not risk her life so foolishly. If I died, she would never make it off this planet alive.

I found a rocky outcropping and moved out of sight of the structure. Gently placing Abby on her feet, I pointed to a small overhang that would hide her well. "Crawl under those rocks and wait for me."

"Are you kidding me? You're going to leave me out here alone?"

"There may be hostiles inside the building. I won't risk your life."

"But you'll risk yours?" She shuddered. "I don't like this. Why can't we just stay here and wait for someone to track down the escape pod? Would we be able to see a ship from here?"

"Yes. But they also could be flying into a trap."

"Great. Why can't I ever win an argument with you?"

"Because I am your much older, much wiser mate who is very skilled in all types of battle."

"Arguing isn't a battle."

"Is it not?" I was glad she could not see my grin as I detected a hint of irritation overcoming her fear. That was good. Angry was better than afraid. "You will remain here while I make sure it is safe."

"Bossy. Except I don't like it this time."

Unexpected laughter burst through me. I pulled her to my chest and massaged her back through her suit. "Pretend we are playing hide and seek." The thought of our last game made my cock hard and my breathing shorten. I stepped back and pointed to her hiding place. "But this time, count to ten thousand."

"Is that supposed to be funny?" she grumbled as she dropped to her hands and knees and crawled under the rocks.

"Very." I could not resist watching her ass wiggle, recalling how her hot pussy felt wrapped around my cock, as she scrambled into place.

"I can feel you looking at me."

"I like the view."

"You have a terrible sense of humor. Has anyone ever told you that?"

"Many times."

"Of course they have. You're a caveman."

"Then it is a good thing you like cave males."

"You're the first." She huffed. "And there you go again, winning an argument. I'm going to have to work on my strategy." Her sigh was audible. "But then, there are all the orgasms. Gives you a massive advantage."

I laughed again, shocked at how one small, sassy female could so completely change my life. I did not laugh. I did not play games. I did not speak to females outside my duties to my legion. Abby was changing everything. "I will be back, Abby, once I know it is safe. Do not fear and do not move from this place."

"Ten thousand? You're crazy, you know that?"

Once Abby disappeared from view, I turned back and closed the distance to the abandoned structure. The base was in worse condition than I'd thought. Up close, it was easy to see the distinctive markings on the Hive structures. They made everything in patterns, usually multiples of three. Even the walls were etched with their odd geometric designs. Massive boot prints covered the ground, some so large only an Atlan in beast mode could have made them.

Had there been a battle here? Perhaps the Hive had held off the Coalition forces just long enough to escape? Or maybe they had decided the base was of no use and abandoned it by choice.

I approached the doors, shocked when the doors slid open to allow me entrance. Blaster in hand, I stepped into darkness. The built-in lights on my suit cut rays of white through the shadows.

Same set of footprints in here. Some Atlan sized, others not. None of this made any sense.

I moved to the control panel and thanked the gods I had scavenged enough Hive tech to recognize some of the switches and scanners. I turned on life support to the room, enabled the shield on the front doors and waited until I heard the telltale hiss of fresh air being pumped into the room from the atmospheric generators. The Hive were a mindless horde, but they were extremely good at keeping their new puppets alive.

In just a few minutes, I had scanned the entire base

for movement, energy or anything that would indicate activity. Nothing.

Satisfied it would be safe for Abby, I ran back to where I had left her.

"Abby, it is safe."

Her head popped out from under the rock. "Nine thousand, nine hundred and thirty-six."

I reached down and pulled her out of her hiding spot. "Found you."

"Nine thousand, nine hundred and thirty-seven."

"Abby."

"I'm on a roll here. I've never counted this high before."

"Do you wish to continue? I will wait."

"No. My brain is tired of numbers. Took you long enough."

"My apologies, mate. I had to ensure the Hive base was truly abandoned."

"The Hive?"

"Yes."

"Oh shit." Abby bent over, her hands resting on her knees as she took several deep breaths. "The Hive. That's so not cool."

"You are safe with me."

"I know." She held out one of her hands toward me, and I ignored it, choosing instead to lift her into my arms once more. "Doesn't mean I won't be totally freaked out."

"Perhaps I need to use my large...*advantage* to fill your pussy and distract you with orgasms."

"Tease. There is no way we are having sex in some dusty, old, abandoned Hive place. That's creepy."

"Is this an argument, mate?"

Abby burst into laughter, and my heart soared. "No. Definitely not."

"I think it is."

"No. Not an argument."

"Yes."

"No."

I laughed as I carried her the rest of the way to the Hive base.

11

Abby, Abandoned Hive Base, Latiri 4

Creepy? Totally.

Dusty? Yes. But more than dust, there was debris everywhere. Broken things. Forgotten things. It looked like whoever had been here had just looked up one day, turned around and walked out.

The place was like a strange ghost town. Buttons still blinked different colors on multiple screens and panels. Weird noises came from out of nowhere to freak me out. All of the writing was strange. Thanks to my NPU, if I stared at it long enough, the meaning would kind of drift into my mind like a soft breeze brushing past my brain. The sensation was weird as hell, but I was thankful for it. Seeing controls for elevators and life support didn't scare me as much as looking at a bunch of alien symbols would have. Cormac stood nearby, at another section of the control room, probably looking over weapons or something. Maybe trying to send a message? I had no idea.

"This is unreal."

"I wish that were true, mate. I would never bring you to a place such as this."

"I don't mind. I think it's amazing." I was in an alien base. On an alien planet. In another part of the galaxy with the sexiest, hottest, most protective male I'd ever met. And he was mine. I still had to pinch myself to believe it. Everything in my life had changed. Everything.

So. Damn. Cool. Scary, but amazing. I knew if Cormac was not with me, I would be terrified. Thankfully, I didn't have to worry about that. The man—alien—barely allowed me out of his sight.

Thank god. I really didn't want to die from a terror-induced heart attack before I was twenty.

Using my gloved hand to clear away more of the console I stood over, I studied the flickering lights and tried to intuit more alien language.

"Gods be damned, the comm controls are encrypted."

"Can you break the code or bypass it or something?" Wiping away another small section of debris, I looked over my shoulder to find him scowling at me.

"I am a warrior and an assassin. Enforcer, smuggler, occasionally, a thief. This is not something I can do. I am sorry, mate. I have failed you. We will have to hope the escape pod's beacon leads Styx to us."

His shoulders slumped, and he looked...upset? I

needed to distract him. I couldn't stand to see him chastising himself so harshly for something neither of us could do. Holding my hand out to him, I tilted my head and willed him to see the smile inside my helmet. "Come here, mate. We are still alive. Neither one of us is hurt. This has been an incredible adventure so far. You have taken excellent care of me."

"You should be safe on Rogue 5." Despite his protest, he walked toward me and took my hand. I pulled him as close as I could get him, content when his arm came around me and his hand rested on my hip. God, his hands were big.

I loved his hands. What he could do with them.

Focus, Abby.

I cleared my throat. "Tell me what these controls can do. I think this is the life support? I think it says something about the air?" I pointed to the blinking lights I'd uncovered. "Air would be great. I'd love to take off this helmet and kiss you."

Cormac squeezed my bottom before leaning over the control panel, placing his hands palm down as he inspected the massive area. This section took up almost the entire wall on this side of the room. It had to be at least three times as long as I was tall. And for an abandoned place, there were a lot of lights still on.

My mate went still. Too still. I reached for his bicep and wrapped both hands around it. "What is it? You're scaring me."

"This can't be." He used both hands to clear larger

sections of the controls. Forced to let go of him or be swung around like a wet towel, I stepped to the side to give him a bit more room. I could still see the panel, but I had no idea what had him so rattled.

"What?"

"There are multiple subterranean levels. That is to be expected. But this..." He pointed to a section near the top. Every light was on. Different colors. But every single one was flickering or flashing or just shining like a light bulb. "This should not be."

I leaned up on tip-toe to get a closer look at the symbols etched into the panel and waited impatiently for my NPU to figure out how to communicate the meaning to my brain. One moment I had no idea, and the next...

"Prisoners? Does that say something about a prison?"

"Yes." Cormac spun around and grabbed his gear, throwing everything he'd just removed, his pack, rifle and second rifle, back into place on his large frame. "I'm going down there."

"Who would they have down there?"

Cormac took several steps toward what looked like elevator doors at the far end of the room. I chased after him like a hungry kitten. "Wait."

"You will remain here with the doors locked."

I shook my head before he finished his sentence. "No way. It's creepy in here. Besides, what if whoever blew up your ship finds us before Styx does? I'd be up here alone."

"Fuck." Cormac slammed his palm against the

elevator door. It was a dark gray, like pencil lead, not shiny like the elevator doors on Earth. As if the elevator heard him, the doors slipped open the moment his hand lifted. "Do you have your blaster?"

"Yes."

"Stay behind me. Do everything I tell you to do. Do you understand?"

"Yes." I did not want to get between my mate and anything he thought needed killing, that was for sure. I was short. I wasn't stupid.

Cormac gently placed me behind him as the elevator doors closed in front of us. I was expecting a sinking feeling in the pit of my stomach like I experienced on elevators at home. This was ten times worse. We were falling at exactly the speed needed to keep my toes touching the floor, but the stopping was really going to be rough.

"Cormac!"

He grabbed me at once, turning his back to the door and holding me to his chest as the elevator slammed to a stop. He absorbed the shock easily. Had he not been holding me, I would have crumpled into a mess. One, I wasn't as strong as he was. Two, my balance was far from gymnast level. I would have been on my ass. Probably slammed my head into the wall. Sheesh.

"What kind of stupid elevator is this?"

"Hive. Their limbs have been enhanced to withstand much more than their normal biology would allow." Cormac released me, using one hand to ensure I was steady enough to stand on my own as he turned back around to face the doors. He completely blocked my view, but I didn't try to peek around him. Nope. I'd stare at his magnificent ass instead. Not monsters. Damn it.

All I could think about was a stupid movie I'd seen as a kid. One of the science fiction movies that had *Star something* in the title. They'd had these evil enemies that flew around space in giant cubes. They were half human and half robot, and their queen had a squiggly robot spine that came out of her body and twisted around like a worm. Disgusting.

I'd had nightmares for weeks. Was that what the Hive was? I was beginning to think maybe I should have stayed up top and taken my chances.

Dim light filled the corridor beyond us. Cormac stepped forward, and I followed, staying about three steps behind him. A loud thumping noise came from up ahead, like someone was hitting a mound of dirt with a baseball bat. Every few seconds...*thump.*

I wanted to ask Cormac what that could be, but he was moving like a ghost, so quiet if I couldn't see him right in front of me, I wouldn't believe he was there.

We came to the end of the short corridor, and Cormac turned to his right, blaster raised. I froze, waiting to see what would happen.

Thump...thump...thump.

"Fuck." Cormac put his blaster back into its holster on the side of his suit and cursed some more. He looked over to me and motioned for me to come closer. I moved to his side as fast as I could manage. I looked down the new corridor and felt my heart sink into my stomach.

There were prison cells. Rows and rows and rows of them as far as I could see. Five cells on either side of this area each held giant aliens I recognized at once. Atlans. Like my friend Elena's mate, Tane. Atlan Warlords. Except these all had metal on their bodies or sunk into their skin like tattoos. Every Atlan had his eyes trained on Cormac. Wary. All but one.

THUMP.

The Atlan in the center on my right slammed his fist into some kind of energy field that made up the front of their prison cells. His knuckles were bloody, some so mangled I could see bone.

"Don't worry about him. He'll stop soon. Eat. Sleep. Wake up and destroy his other hand." The voice came from the first cell on the left. Cormac turned to face the Atlan. "His name is Stryck, but we just call him Thumper."

"Like the rabbit from *Bambi*?" I blurted out.

The Atlan who had spoken focused on me, and I stepped closer to Cormac. Holy crap, these guys were huge. Yes, Tane and the others I'd met were big, too. But I knew them. Knew they were good guys. Being stared at by an angry Atlan who had been left to rot in a prison cell? Not fun.

"What is this place?" Cormac asked him.

"Obvious, isn't it?"

"Why are you here?" Cormac asked. "Why did they leave you here?"

The Atlan on my right answered. He was obviously in beast mode because he was huge. His jaw was too pronounced, and he had to bend his neck to prevent his head from hitting the ceiling when he stood up from his matt on the floor and walked toward the front of his cell. "Break us."

"I don't understand. What good does it do to lock you up when they aren't even here?"

"Be back."

"Fuck." Cormac lifted his hands and removed his helmet. I did the same, thankful for new air to breathe. It wasn't exactly fresh, but it was better than the hot air inside my helmet. I was really tired of smelling my own breath.

THUMP.

The repetitive sound had not broken its cadence. I looked at the broken, bloodied hand of the offender once more and shuddered. If the Hive left them here to make them lose their minds, it appeared to be working, at least on one of them.

Cormac walked to stand before the first Atlan who had spoken. I wandered a couple steps farther down the corridor and craned my neck to see what lay beyond. More cells. Were they all full of Atlans? Did they have other alien species in here?

I kept moving, and my jaw dropped. *That* was definitely *not* an Atlan, or anything I would consider human.

Human-ish, maybe? Except its head was too long. Its fingertips ended in long claws that looked sharp enough to slice silk, and its eyes were an odd color. What was that color? Key lime green? Like the pie? "Cormac?"

He was at my side at once. "Gods be damned. How the fuck did they find you?"

The creature lifted its head to look at us and then rose from the floor to a standing position. He wore pants that had been ripped above his knees and nothing else. Cords of muscle that looked like twisted ropes covered every inch of his body. His chest was massive, his thighs bigger around than my hips. He was just as big as the Atlans, but he had fangs longer than Cormac's. Sharper, too. And his voice, when he spoke, sounded like rolling gravel. "Cormac."

"Ruk?" Cormac dipped his chin in some kind of odd bow. "How did the Hive get their hands on you?"

Cormac knew this one? The one with the fangs?

Of course he did.

"Siren scum. They are trading captives to the Hive for weapons."

Cormac visibly paled, and he raised a hand to his chest as if his heart hurt.

Who was this guy?

The thought seemed to draw the creature's attention to me. He took his time looking me over, head to toe like I was some kind of insect he'd never seen before. "Your mate?"

"Yes."

"This female is too fragile. Too small. You should have mated my sister, as the elders ordered."

"What?" I looked from the alien to Cormac. "What is he talking about?"

Cormac cleared his throat. "This is Rukzi. He is a Hyperion chieftain's son and a friend. Everyone on Rogue 5 has Hyperion ancestry."

I looked from Cormac to Rukzi, who bowed slightly at the waist and was still at least two heads taller than me. He was even taller than Cormac.

"Many blessings, female."

"Rukzi, this is Abby. She is human, from a planet they call Earth, and she is my mate."

"Yessss." Rukzi's voice was almost a hiss. "I can smell that." He glanced back down at me. "I suppose it is too late to undo what has been done."

"Yes. She is mine."

Undo it? Undo what? Me?

That. Was. It. "You, Rukzi, are rude." I crossed my arms over my chest and glared. Hard. "And disrespectful."

Rukzi looked at me through the energy barrier for a count of three, then burst out laughing, the sound more like a huge lion's roar than a chuckle. "Very well, female. You have courage. I approve. You may call me Ruk." He looked back at Cormac. "Although I shall not inform my sister of your match. I will leave that to you. She will be very disappointed."

"So you have said, as she's welcoming the strongest warriors in your clan to her bed every night."

"She chooses well, indeed." Ruk sounded proud of her, as if sleeping with a different man—alien warrior —every night was not only normal, but admired. "Perhaps now that you are"—he looked at me again—"mated, she will choose to have a child and make our clan stronger. My sister will give us exceptional warriors."

Wow. These guys were a lot different from any of the uptight assholes I'd known on Earth. I told my dad I'd lost my virginity at sixteen just to see if he'd blow a blood vessel. He'd lectured me for an hour, but his arteries and veins had remained intact.

THUMP.

I jumped at the sound and realized I had completely tuned out the other prisoners.

Cormac stepped forward and moved his hand over some kind of scanner on the wall right next to Ruk's cell. The barrier disappeared, and Ruk stepped forward to offer his hand to Cormac. The two grasped each other's forearms like fighters in a gladiator movie, and I took a step back behind Cormac. Now that Ruk was free, he stood to his full height.

Shit. He was a *lot* taller than Cormac. His hands were too close to eye level, which meant I heard the mushy sound of flesh moving as he retracted those ridiculous claws like a cat. Other than being a giant and having eyes the color of that disgusting pie, he looked almost normal. He smiled—I think it was a smile—when he caught me staring.

Normal? Hah. How the hell had I forgotten those fangs? This guy would give a vampire nightmares.

"We appreciate the little family reunion, but can you get us the fuck out of here?" The first Atlan's frustration was clear in his sharp tone.

Cormac turned to me and held my gaze. I knew when I saw the stress lines around his eyes and mouth that I was not going to like whatever it was he was about to say.

My mate walked to stand before the Atlan's cell and shook his head. "You are all covered in Hive tech. You admit being placed here because you have been battling Hive mind control and they are trying to break you down mentally. I have no idea what you will do once you are released. I give you my word I will notify Commander Karter of your predicament as soon as our rescue team arrives and I have a working comm."

The Atlan punched the barrier seconds before his friend in the other cell. The two thumping sounds created a rhythm like listening to a heartbeat. *Thump-thump.* "Are you fucking kidding me, rogue?"

"No. I must protect my mate, and I do not know you or your comrades. I would be outnumbered and unable to protect her from all of you. I will not take that risk."

"Fuck." The Atlan looked down at me, and his gaze softened just enough. "You are human, from the same world as Lady Deston, the queen of Prillon Prime?"

"Yes." I'd read about her and Leah, the woman who was now queen of another planet called Viken. Every woman on Earth who volunteered for the Interstellar

Brides Program knew they had a chance to be a real-life queen or princess. Me? I'd just wanted a mate who loved me and put me first. So far, Cormac had done exactly that.

"Is your mate an honorable male?"

Why the hell was this Atlan asking me? I was a social media goddess. I lied for a living. If he believed humans didn't lie, he was in for one hell of a shock someday. Thankfully, I could tell him the absolute truth. "Yes. He is the best man I know. He saved my li—"

Cormac stepped forward and interrupted me before I could complete my sentence or make my own vow to these Atlans. "You have my word, Warlord. That is all I can do. The S-Gen machines that have kept you alive this long should continue functioning until help arrives."

"And how long will that be?"

"A day, two at most."

The Atlan looked from Cormac to me, this time holding my gaze. "I am Warlord Enzu, my lady. Please tell Commander Karter to hurry." He glanced down the corridor as his fellow prisoner punched the energy field again. Same rhythm. Steady. Like the drip from a faucet. It was like that Altan was so far gone he didn't even realize we were here.

"We will tell him. I promise."

"Very well."

If necessary, I would find this Commander Karter and tell him about this place myself. However, if Cormac did not believe it was safe to free the Atlans now, I would not argue. They did have strange things that looked like they had been melted into their bodies. Fused, or maybe implanted? Some were on their heads or faces. A lot of these Atlans had them on their arms or legs. Some of them on their spines. None of them were wearing shirts, so their massive forms were on display.

Sure, I was mated, but I wasn't dead, and Atlans were hotties. But were those oddly colored gray and silver bits the Hive tech Cormac was referring to? If so, Ruk had some on his body, too. In fact, he wasn't far off from the creepy cube lady with her wormy neck. Ruk's spine was completely covered as far as I could see, from his waist to the back of his head. Not good.

But Cormac knew him personally. They had history. Cormac obviously respected and trusted him. We had found Cormac's friend locked in an underground prison on an uninhabited trash heap of a planet with a bunch of Atlan prisoners.

Holy crap, outer space was crazy. And I'd been away from Earth for less than a week.

Cormac placed his hand on my lower back. "Let's go, Abby."

I was still looking at Enzu. "I don't like leaving them."

Enzu's voice was gentle. "It is all right, Abby. We understand. The safety of a mate must always come first. We have spent countless weeks here. We can survive a couple more days."

I shook my head as I walked away. Cormac followed, placing himself between Ruk and me. On the way up in the elevator, Cormac pressed me to the side of the wall, his body squared off with our new friend. I couldn't see anything except Cormac's back, but that was fine by me.

"Helmet on, Abby."

"What about Ruk?" I slipped the stuffy helmet back over my head and listened to the sound of it sealing me in, the faint hiss of air. Cormac put his helmet on as well.

"Do not worry about me. I am tougher than I look."

Good god, I hoped not.

The elevator doors opened, and the sound of blaring alarms was so loud it hurt my ears. Cormac pressed me to the wall, trapping me in place behind his bulk.

"What the fuck?" He turned around and placed his hand just below my neck. "You stay here, Abby." Cormac moved to step out of the elevator, but Ruk placed his hand on Cormac's shoulder and held him back.

"No. I will go. Stay here. Protect your mate." Long claws slid out from the tips of his fingers, the sickening sound of tearing flesh nearly making me gag. I blinked, and he was gone.

12

Cormac

*S*tay behind. Protect my mate. I hated every word. Gods be damned; I knew Ruk was right. My first duty was to Abby. I would have offered him one of my rifles, but I knew he would have laughed at me, that low, rolling laugh that had always reminded me of wild things and thick forest. Many of the people on Rogue 5 had forgotten our ancestors, at least the Hyperion half. The savage half.

The stronger half.

Trying to use one of my weapons would only slow him down.

He could move even faster than an Elite Hunter from Everis when in a fight. I'd seen it many times during my visits to Hyperion. It was the reason he was the heir to his clan's chieftain and the reason he had his choice of sex partners among their females. He rarely turned down any female's invitation, yet he had not chosen a mate.

Although, judging by the way he had taken an instant liking to my Abby, Ruk's unmated status might soon be coming to an end. Although if my friend wanted a female from Earth, he was going to have to figure out how to get there. It was rare for anyone from Rogue 5 to mate a human. But a Hyperion? As far as I knew, Ruk was the first full-blooded Hyperion ever to leave the planet.

A horrendous roar came from the direction of the control room Abby and I had been in earlier.

Fuck. That was Ruk, and he was in full battle mode.

I hit the elevator button and stepped outside, both blasters out and ready.

"Cormac!" Abby shouted from behind me as the doors began to slide closed.

"Go below. I will come for you when it's safe." I twisted to face her and tapped the side of my helmet to prevent her protest. "You will be able to hear me, mate. Now go!"

The door closed completely. Abby was safely out of harm's way.

I ran toward the sounds of fighting, eager to find out what the fuck was going on. I hoped our attackers were Siren scum and not Hive. I'd faced off with the Coalition's enemy before and had no desire to do so again. Killing what had once been an honorable warrior seemed wrong somehow.

Killing an asshole was much easier.

Not that it mattered. I would kill a king to keep Abby safe.

Reaching the control room, I slid to a stop.

Fuck.

It was the Hive.

I stepped over the dead bodies of two Hive Scouts, identifiable by their smaller size. The Scouts were hard to deal with. The Soldiers were damn near impossible unless you had the high ground or a group of Atlan warlords fighting on your side.

I had neither, but I rushed for the main entrance. Ruk had chosen the doorway to make his stand. With the narrow entrance, he could control how many of the Hive he had to fight at once.

"How many?" I yelled.

"Twelve," Ruk yelled back moments before crouching low to dodge a blaster shot. Claws extended, he swiped at the abdomen of the Hive Soldier nearest him. By his angular features and copper-colored skin, I knew that Soldier had been a Prillon warrior. No more. The Soldier's armor gave way, and his gut ripped open at the force of Ruk's attack. The Hive Soldier didn't even blink. It was as if he felt nothing. No pain. No emotion. Nothing. He just kept coming.

By the gods, I fucking hated fighting these things.

I moved to position several steps behind Ruk, my rifle pointed at the doors. I was an excellent shot. When Ruk ducked or moved to either side, I would take out as many of them as I could.

I had my opening before I even had my feet set on the floor. I fired.

Direct hit. The bright energy from the ion blast enveloped the Hive Soldier's entire head. As quickly as the light exploded, it was gone. The Hive Soldier remained. Completely intact.

Again and again I fired. Head. Chest. Legs. Nothing worked. It was like I was simply shining a light in their direction.

They should have gone down with the first hit.

"Fuck!"

"New armor!" Ruk shouted. "Blasters won't work."

"New armor. New fucking armor." Dropping my blasters at my feet, I pulled my knives free from their sheaths, one on each thigh.

"Cormac?" Abby's panicked voice filled my helmet. "Cormac? Are you all right? What's happening?"

I didn't dare tell her the truth. Ruk and I were facing off with the strongest fighters the Hive could produce, and we were down at least six to one.

But I had adaptive armor, too. Their blaster shots would hurt, but they wouldn't take me down. And Ruk? Those ion blasts would do little more than make him angry.

Six to one. I liked those odds.

"Everything is fine, Abby. Our arrival must have triggered a sensor."

"A Hive sensor?"

"Yes. Stay put. Ruk and I are handling it. I'm turning off my comms. I'll come get you when it's over."

I couldn't afford to be distracted by her voice at a critical moment. I had to kill these fuckers as quickly as possible and get her out of here before more of them showed up.

bby

"**S**hit. Shit. Shit." I paced in front of Enzo's prison cell. I knew that if I had to, I could release him. I was fairly confident he would protect me. Not one hundred percent, but like ninety-five. That was pretty good.

Stryck, aka Thumper, was still going strong. The *thump, thump, thump* did absolutely nothing to calm my frazzled nerves. The elevator ride had been bad enough. I'd grabbed onto anything I could find as the freefall to the lower levels had almost buckled my knees. I'd forgotten what it was like riding in that stupid thing. And it was damn near impossible without Cormac there to help hold me up.

"What is happening?" Enzo asked.

I saw no reason not to tell him. "Apparently we triggered some kind of Hive alarm. Cormac says there are twelve of them, and they have some kind of new armor that he's not too happy about."

"Free us, Abby. Do it now."

"You know I can't do that." Not unless it was the only way to save Cormac. Then I would do it in a heartbeat and take my chances, promise or no promise. I would not allow Cormac to die. No way. He was mine. "This wasn't supposed to happen. None of it." I fought back tears and knew I was going to fail miserably. "Not the stupid bomb or the escape pod or you guys or the stupid Hive. None of it."

"The new Hive armor absorbs the power from an ion blast. Cormac's weapons will be useless against them." Enzo had both palms flat against the energy barrier that separated us. I had to look way, *way* up to look him in the eye.

"How do you know that?"

"How do you think we got here? We were deployed Latiri 7 for a ground assault, and a unit of Hive ambushed us with their new armor. We ripped them to pieces, but there were just too many of them."

"A fucking swarm." Stryck spoke between hits. "I will kill them all."

Oh my god. What was I supposed to do now? Ruk had refused to take a weapon. Cormac had two rifles and a blaster, but what good would that do him against twelve of these Hive things if they all had special armor?

Cormac was big and scary. So was Ruk. But they were two guys fighting a dozen. Shit. Shit. Shit.

"Free us, Abby."

I took a deep breath as I considered my options. An eerie silence enveloped me, and I looked around, realizing every single one of the Atlan prisoners was on his feet at the very edge of the energy fields that trapped them inside their cells...watching me.

Staring, really. Creepy. Intimidating. I had no idea what to do.

"How many of you are there?" I tried to see into the darkened corridor beyond this first section and found I could not.

"There are nine Warlords here. They had others, as well, in the other sections of this place. I do not know how many. But they broke quickly. The Hive took them away, and they did not return."

"But you guys didn't give in?"

"We are Warlords." Enzo spoke those three words as if they would explain everything I needed to know. Luckily for him, I knew Tane and the others on Earth. I knew what a Warlord would do to protect his mate and his people.

"Cormac? Are you there?" I had to give him one more chance. Maybe he had turned his comms back on.

Silence was my only answer.

"Every moment you wait is another you give the Hive to kill your mate."

"Outer space sucks." Cormac was going to yell at me,

but I was going with my ninety-five percent gut instinct that told me Enzo and the rest of these Atlans were good guys. I did not want him to die up there with Ruk. "Okay. But I have one condition."

"As do I, if we are to risk our lives in this battle."

We discussed. We made our bargain.

I lifted my hand to the controls next to Enzo's cell.

13

Cormac

*B*right blood coated the exterior of my armored suit with a layer of sludge. I glanced at Ruk as the remaining Hive Soldiers backed away from us, their footsteps in unison.

That was not right. Not fucking right.

"What are they doing?" Ruk asked.

"I don't know."

"I thought you had faced this enemy."

"I have. Never seen them do this." The Hive Soldiers moved backward in an arc formation but remained facing us. Like me, they had given up on using their ion blasters. Every hit made Ruk more enraged, and the shots glanced off or were absorbed by my armor. Which I suspected was nearly identical to the armor the Hive wore.

This was Styx legion armor. We'd developed it in secret. Kept it quiet.

Someone had sold us out. Worse, they'd sold the new tech to the Hive.

Probably the same fuckers who were rounding up Hyperion natives like Ruk and selling them to the Hive. For what, the gods only knew.

Ruk glared at the retreating enemy and bared his fangs with a roar of challenge. There were seven of them left. We'd managed to take out the Scouts and five of the Soldiers. If I wasn't mistaken, there was an Integration Unit, one of their evil doctors who did all the implantations and torture, standing a good distance behind them. Waiting.

"That fucker in the back is mine."

"He leave you in that cell?"

"He did. I will tear out his throat."

No argument from me. But we had seven Hive Soldiers standing between us and Ruk's prize. Unmoving. Blank expressions. Waiting for...something.

My Hunter blood kicked in and with it the gifts of instinct and heightened senses. I heard the new arrival before I saw it. The mid-sized cargo ship appeared half a minute later. The ship was coming in our direction, the body style not one I recognized, which meant it wasn't legion or Coalition. Fuck. Had to be Hive.

Ruk noticed it, too. "Reinforcements?"

"Looks like."

Ruk lowered his gaze to look over the remaining

Soldiers on the ground several paces in front of us. "Guess we'd better finish them off before their friends get here."

"You go right, I go left?" I asked.

"Meet you in the middle." Ruk charged the far right of their line as I ran toward the Soldier on the far left. Both knives out, I leaped into the air as an ion blaster hit me from the side. The energy bolt stung but did no real damage. Score another win for Styx armor. The fact that the Hive had our tech was a fucking nightmare I couldn't think about right now.

I landed on the ground and rolled on my shoulder. Coming up in a crouch just to the left of the Soldier's boots, I drove my blade up through his groin, going deep.

The Soldier cried out, bending over in agony.

I lifted my remaining knife as his head dropped low and slit his throat.

Blood spilled in a hot flood when I pulled the knife free of his body, giving my blade an extra twist on the way out to make sure this fucker bled to death before any of his friends could save him. The Hive had no mercy, no remorse, no conscience. They would give no quarter. Neither would I.

In the corner of my vision, I saw Ruk's first target fall. He bellowed as he moved on to the next. "I'm coming for you, Four-seven-two. I will bathe in your blood!"

The Soldiers fought viciously, but they were not fighting for anything or anyone. They did not have a mate to protect. A brother who needed them. A legion that needed to be warned about our stolen armor.

They did not have a low-life traitor to hunt.

I rolled and dodged and fought like the monster all of Rogue 5 had named me. I would not lose because I could not. Rage boiled in my blood at the thought that they would harm Abby. That fury gave me speed. Strength. Power. I was Hyperion and Prillon and Everian. I would not fail.

The two Soldiers I faced took turns trying to draw me close. Surround me. Get their hands on me. But I was Hunter fast. Hyperion fast. I did not have to wait the split second it took their bodies to receive their orders from whatever kind of group mind controlled them. The delay made them slow enough to kill.

The first I knocked to the ground. I drove my boot through his helmet to crush his head. His skull cracked and shattered beneath my heel like an oversized egg as I drove my boot all the way to the ground.

The death of his friend seemed to stun the other. I took the opportunity to move in close and shove my knife up under his ribs and into his heart.

With a roar, I twisted the blade before I pulled it free. Time to kill another. And another. And another. I would not stop until Abby was safe.

The ground was littered with Hive dead. Looking for Ruk, I found him chasing down the Integration Unit he'd sworn to kill.

"Leave him. We have incoming!" The ship we'd

spotted earlier looked to be just a few minutes from landing.

"He is mine!" Ruk was the fastest creature on two legs I had ever seen. The Integration Unit Ruk had called Four-seven-two had a significant head start. Ruk caught him in seconds, lifted him by his head and bent the Hive's body nearly in half to expose his throat.

I turned away before Ruk could rip through flesh with his fangs. I didn't need to see that. I fought. I killed. But not with claws and fangs.

But killing was killing. Thinking I was more civilized about it was a head game I didn't need to play. We were the same, Ruk and I. The fucking exact same.

I didn't know how Abby even allowed me to touch her. She was everything I was not. But gods be damned if I was going to give her up now.

Leaving Ruk to his vengeance, I gathered weapons and anything useful I could grab from the Hive corpses. There wasn't much, but anything I could give my legion's scientists and engineers might be helpful. I also made sure to record everything I saw with my helmet's comm system. Maybe the researchers could find a clue as to who had betrayed our legion on one of these dead Soldiers' bodies.

I stashed the ion blasters inside the base entrance and turned as Ruk came back inside. No more than a few minutes had passed. We both turned to watch as the Hive ship slowly descended to the ground. Twenty-one Hive

Soldiers and nine Scouts emerged, wearing the same fucking armor.

Ruk looked at me. "I think it's time to let the Atlans come out to play."

"Fuck." He was right. We were not going to survive without help. "I'll go." I turned my comm back on. "Abby, can you hear me?"

"Yes. God! Thank god you're all right. Are you all right?"

Covered in blood, facing down certain death, I grinned. My Abby, my mate. She was everything. "Yes, but we need help up here. Release the Atlans."

"Too late." Abby's voice sounded a bit too sweet. She was up to something.

"What does that mean, mate?"

Abby's voice was crystal clear in my helmet comm, as was her soft laughter. "I already did."

I turned as the elevator door slid open, and Abby stepped out with Enzo, the one they called Thumper and seven other Atlans.

Ruk looked as well. "Not going to do us much good like that."

I assumed he was referring to the fact that not one of the Atlans was in beast mode. They looked like standard Atlan males.

Enzo caught my eye and grinned as they all filed out. "Had to fit in the elevator."

Abby

I ran to Cormac and wrapped my arms around his waist. He was covered in muck and gross things I didn't want to think about, but I didn't care. The only thing I cared about was that he was alive.

Standing in Cormac's embrace, I glanced over at Ruk, who was watching us as if fascinated. He was literally drenched in blood. His mouth and chin looked like he hadn't just been killing, but eating the enemy as well. Which was just gross. I must have made a face because he opened his mouth to bare his fangs at me. Then he smiled as if everything was right in the world.

"That's a good look on you, Ruk," I teased.

"Indeed. I believe so as well."

"Comfort your mate later, Rogue. They are nearly

upon us." Enzo bent to pick up one of the blasters. Cormac cleared his throat.

"Those won't do any damage. They have modified armor."

Enzo looked Ruk over as I had and then turned to look at something outside on the ground. I craned to see, but Cromac turned his body away and took me with him.

"You do not want to see that, Abby."

"But—"

Enzo's voice was loud enough for me to hear. "He is right. No female should see this." His voice had a tone to it that made me think he was smiling. "Excellent work. Perhaps you are not a complete loss, Rogue."

"Do not praise the pirate. I am winning. I have destroyed six of our enemy. Cormac only three." I heard that rumbling, loud laughter again and couldn't hold back my smile. Ruk was big and scary, but he was growing on me.

"The battle is not over, Ruk." Cormac squeezed me gently as he bantered with his friend.

"It's not?" Oh shit. Glancing down at the floor, I studied the bodies of two of what must be the Hive I'd heard so much about. They looked like normal men, maybe even from Earth or a planet just like ours. But they had even more of the metal in their bodies than the Atlans did, each piece somehow sticking out of the armor. Maybe their armor was designed that way. I didn't know, but their blood was red. The metallic smell of it filled my head and lungs until I struggled to breathe. The bodies were twisted, sliced and torn to pieces. Instinctively, I knew those were Ruk's kills. If there was more of the same outside, the guys were right. I did *not* want to see it.

I stiffened, and Cormac spread his hand over my back like a warm blanket. His size and strength calmed me enough to get over the light-headed, spinning sensation that had sneaked up on me. I was not freaking fainting in front of all these gigantic alpha male warriors. Not happening.

Cormac looked down into my eyes as well as he could through our helmets. "Another ship has arrived. Do not worry, Abby. With the Atlans here, we will easily defeat them."

"How many?" I had not signed up for gore and blood and battles. Hot sex? Hell, yes. A mate totally devoted to me? Double yes. Being scared out of my damn mind? No. I'd kept it together so far, even when our ship was about to explode and we had to cram into the escape pod. This —I looked at the twisted, bloody, Hive corpses one more time—this was over the edge. I began to shake, anxiety making my chest hurt.

With Cormac blocking my view of the entrance, I couldn't see much, but I *could* see five of the Atlans, including Stryck—Thumper. His knuckles were a bloody mess, but he inclined his head to me and began to *change*.

I knew the Atlans on Earth, the ones sent to do the Bachelor Beast television show. Tane, the last one to be mated, had chosen one of my only friends in the world to be his. He was amazing. Elena was totally in love. And I'd seen him in beast mode before. But for fun, mostly. Not like this.

Never like this.

The Atlans transformed into their massive beast forms; that was fine. It was the death I saw in their eyes that made my heart jerk like someone was kicking it with pointed boots every time it dared to beat.

Stryck moved out of my line of sight, and the others followed. I heard one booming order that I assumed came from him. "MOVE!"

Ruk took a step toward the back with his clawed hands raised, palms out. "Go ahead. I already got mine."

"Got your what?" I asked.

"Vengeance."

Cormac lifted my feet off the floor and walked toward the elevator.

"No. I am not going back down there. No way."

"You will be safe there, Abby."

"Not if they win. And I'd rather not be trapped underground if they kill all of you."

"No one will touch you." His vow made the hair on the back of my neck stand up. I believed him.

"Then I'm perfectly safe up here."

Cormac stopped moving and looked down at me. "Stubborn female. You are just like Harper."

"Good. Then we'll be best friends."

Cormac chuckled as he lifted me onto the top of one

of the large control stations. "Do you have your weapons?"

"All set." I showed him my knife with one hand and my baby blaster with the other.

"Their armor protects them from blaster fire. If you must use it, aim for their head."

"Okay." I scooted back as far as I could get. I didn't have a direct line of sight out the entrance, but I could see a little bit of ground. I could hear the Atlans roaring like a pack of wild monsters. I pressed myself flat—less of a target—and told Cormac to go.

The control room was empty. Ruk must have followed the Atlans outside.

"Cormac?"

"Yes, mate?" He turned his head to look at me.

"I love you, okay? So don't die."

He froze as if stunned. I waited for him to say it back, for him to say *anything*, but he simply turned and ran out to join the battle.

Lying to myself—and knowing it—I tried to convince myself that I didn't care if he said the words or not. He took care of me. He pledged to protect me and never leave me. I could make him fall in love with me eventually, right? In fact, thinking I actually loved him already was probably stupid hormones. And orgasms. And the whole *you have shared trauma* thing. Like almost dying tied us together with some kind of cosmic bond.

I tried not to move. I tried not to listen to the sounds coming from outside. I did pretty well on the first goal.

Horribly on the second. I was trying, in vain, not to picture bodies being ripped to shreds—especially Cormac's—when I heard clattering on the floor *inside* the control room.

As slowly as possible, I scooted toward the edge of my perch and looked down.

Oh, shit.

What were those things?

Three of them. About the size of a three- or four-year-old child crawling on all fours, the creatures had the silver and gray Hive tech along their spines and on top of their heads. Were these Hive, too? Because these things were not any kind of humanoid species. More like over-sized lizards with claws and razor-sharp teeth that each looked at least as long as my thumbs. Their body was covered in scales that looked like an alligator's that had turned to shiny obsidian. Their eyes were silver. Not gray. Silver, like the fork next to my plate at dinner. In the faint light, they moved like shadows, claws clicking and clacking on the flooring as they stuck their heads in every nook and cranny. Sniffed. Hunted.

How good was their sense of smell? If we were talking human-ish, I was probably okay. But dog? Or worse, a bear? I was screwed.

I tightened my grip on both weapons and tried not to make a single sound. I didn't dare call out to Cormac. These things would hear me and be on me before he could get here.

In less than a minute, I had my answer. The creature

nearest me stopped and lifted its head to sniff the air. The others did the same, as if their three minds were connected. Creepy.

As one unit, they turned and stared directly at me.

"Cormac!" I screamed.

They gathered their hind legs to jump.

The center creature leaped at me. Directly in front of me, the black head and snapping jaws just cleared the top. It ripped holes in the material I sat on with its front claws and hung by its front two feet, scrambling to get up with the back two.

By sheer dumb luck, I managed to plunge my knife somewhere in the thing's neck.

Good news, it fell to the floor.

Bad news, it took my knife with it.

The one on my right leaped, the front half of its body joining me on my perch. I rolled to my side, kicking at it with my boot as I fired my ion blaster at the head of the third monster climbing up on my left. It hadn't jumped at me, but it shoved its claws through the panel and was walking up as easily as if there were stairs.

The blaster shots were doing nothing. Barely slowing it down.

I kicked the other off the top, but I knew it would leap back up as soon as it got its feet under it. They were both going to be on me, and I had nothing to fight with.

Shit. Shit. Shit.

15

Cormac

I understood rage. I understood vengeance. I had never seen anything close to this level of savagery as the Atlans settled the score with the Hive who had kept them captive.

Limbs flew in every direction. Arms. Legs. Upper half of a torn and shredded body. Lower half. Literal pieces of the Hive reinforcements that had come off that ship landed around me with solid thuds.

Twice I had to dodge a particularly angry throw by Enzo. Calm on the outside, wrath on the inside.

Fuck me. No wonder Atlan Warlords were the most feared fighters in the galaxy. This wasn't a battle. This was carnage.

I didn't dare step between a beast and any of the Hive.

Not only was I not needed, I wasn't sure some of the beasts were of a mind to recognize friend from foe.

I remained near the entrance to the control room to handle any stragglers that might make their way toward my mate. I'd killed enough for one day. If they needed me, I'd fight. However, the odds of that were looking slim.

"Cormac!"

Ruk's shout drew my attention. He was pointing to the rock cliffs that formed an arc with the base at its center.

Creatures clung to the walls, at least twelve that I could see, with a possibility of more hiding behind rocks or in the shadows. Their bodies black and scaled, they looked small, perhaps knee high. Regardless of their size, they had the silver eyes and integrated circuitry and pieces on their bodies that designated them as part of the Hive.

The Hive was using animals now?

And what the fuck *were* those things? I'd never seen a native creature on any world that looked like this. Perhaps they were from the Hive home world. Wherever that was.

Their claws and teeth looked like they could do some serious damage. If there were a good number of them, and they coordinated their attack with Hive mind control? Not good. Not fucking good at all.

Did the Coalition know about these things?

"You go right. I'll go left?" I yelled to Ruk.

Ruk didn't answer. He sprang at the creature nearest him with a roar.

I didn't have time to see what happened because the creature nearest me chose that moment to attack.

I fired my blaster. Direct hit.

Fuck. They had shields, too.

Three of them surrounded me like a pack on a wild hunt. I didn't have Ruk's claws. I had two knives and a mate to protect.

"Come on!" I yelled at the one in the center. As I'd hoped, it charged me.

Twisting away at the last moment, I drove both knives into its side and threw it at its companion, keeping hold of the knives' handles as the black, scaly body slipped off the blades and then slammed into the second creature. I knew I had only seconds before the one I had buried beneath the carcass of its friend was on its feet again. I turned to face the third, rushing the thing to force a fight.

The animal leaped at me, muzzle going for my throat. I used its momentum against it and slammed us both to the ground, driving my blade through its skull when we landed. I shoved and twisted until I felt ground beneath the tip.

A low screeching sound caused me to look up from where I lay on top of the corpse. Drawing my legs beneath me into a crouched position, I yanked the blade from the skull at my side and held the screeching thing's gaze.

I recognized intelligence there. Frightening. Focused. Furious that I'd murdered two of its friends. "What are you?"

The monster opened its mouth as if to respond, another screech like metal grinding on metal. I shook my head to clear it of the hideous sound.

"Cormac!"

Abby? My mate sounded terrified.

"Abby!" I was out of time.

I rushed the creature in front of me, expecting it to leap for my throat as the other had. As expected, it leaped. Timing my thrust just right, I plunged both blades into its neck as I caught it. Claws raked down my arms from shoulder to elbow. Searing pain exploded where it sliced through my armor, like acid burning through muscle to bone.

"Abby!"

I threw the carcass aside and ran for the entrance of the base. I reached the door in time to see my mate stab one of the creatures climbing toward her.

Another was nearly upon her, snapping at her feet despite the kicks she managed to land on the monster's head. A third climbed up the side of the panel. She hit it in the hide with ion blasts, but the weapon didn't have much effect.

"Cormac." Abby whimpered my name as if she had lost all hope. She hadn't seen me yet. That sound nearly broke me.

Something inside me snapped. I had battled. I had raged. I had killed. This fury was raw. Brutal. Primitive. And it was all for her.

I grabbed the creature snarling at her feet and

slammed its spine down over my knee. The animal's bones snapped and popped. I did not stop, literally ripping the thing in half like an Atlan.

Moving with every ounce of speed in my Hyperion and Hunter blood, I wrapped my hand around the hind leg of the climber and swung a wide arc, slamming the monster's head into the hard floor, over and over until the body went limp. Probably would have kept going out of pure rage that they dared attack my mate, but a soft cry pulled me back to myself.

"Abby, are you hurt?"

"No. I don't think so." Her voice trembled, and I had to strain to hear it.

Turning to put her at my back, my attention on the door in case more of the fuckers slipped inside, I fought to slow my pulse. My breathing. I was holding on to my control by a thread. I'd nearly lost her. Half a second longer and...

Her small hand appeared in my peripheral vision as she reached down to touch my shoulders. "Oh god. You're hurt!"

"I am fine, mate."

"No, you're not. Where is one of those green wand things?"

"The battle is not over, Abby. I will tend the wound when I know you are safe."

I expected her to argue. This was Abby, after all. Instead, she rested her hand just above the wound, as if touching me brought her comfort.

"Okay."

Minutes seemed like hours as I listened to the sounds of the fighting coming to an end. Ruk's raging occurred less and less often. I heard voices speaking to one another rather than the chaos and noise of battle.

Ruk and Stryck of the thumping fists appeared next to one another at the entrance.

"Everything all right in here?" Ruk asked.

"Yes. Is it over?"

"For now," the big Atlan beast responded.

"Did we lose anyone?"

The Atlan snorted at me as if that was a stupid question. Perhaps it was, but I didn't have time to think any more of it because my mate cried out. I turned in time to catch her as she leaped into my arms. She trembled but didn't speak. Expecting a massive explosion of tears, I didn't know what to do with this quiet, shivering female, had no idea how to comfort her.

"Abby?"

"Just don't let go."

"Never." I lifted her into my arms and told her to hide her face in my neck as I walked past the ground covered in blood, body parts and pieces of the dead Hive and their strange creatures. There had been many more than the few I had seen. Many, many more.

The Atlans were moving in and out of the Hive ship. I did not know what they were doing, but they appeared to know how to operate the small transport. Good. Perhaps we could get the fuck off this rock.

I needed to get my mate home to Rogue 5. Safe. Far, far away from the Hive, the Coalition Fleet and this war.

My mate would not suffer this terror again.

bby

*C*ormac's arms were the only two things keeping me from breaking into a million pieces and sobbing until I had no tears left. I'd never been that scared in my life.

Cormac was amazing. Strong. Devoted. Sexy. Kind. Everything I could want in a mate. I was head-over-heels in love with him. Gone. I wanted to be with him forever.

Outer space, however, sucked. Sucked great big, fat, hairy balls.

The Atlans were preparing the Hive ship for takeoff. Cormac probably assumed we would all be going to the same place. But I'd made a promise, and I intended to keep it as Enzo and the Atlans had kept theirs.

Cormac was alive. That had been my condition. No matter what happened, they had to keep him alive. I didn't see the fight. I had no idea what had happened. Cormac was holding me. Right now that was the only thing I cared about.

"Thank you." I lifted my free arm—the other was

locked between his body and my side—and wrapped it around his neck. "You saved my life."

"You are mine, Abby. I will always protect you. Always come for you."

It wasn't exactly *I love you,* but I'd take it. For now.

Cormac's arms had pretty much stopped bleeding where one of those things had clawed him to shreds. Now there were fresh red wet spots staggered her and there. "Do the Hive have those green wand things?"

"I have one stored in my suit."

"What?" I slapped my hand against his chest. "You put me down right now. Are you kidding me?"

Cormac kept walking toward the Hive ship.

"No. Put. Me. Down."

He stopped but did not release me. Instead, he tightened his arms around me and lowered his head until our helmets connected. "I need you close, Abby. I need you safe in my arms."

Sweet. It really was, but I was a practical girl in all the ways that counted. "And I need to take care of you. You are injured and in pain."

"The pain is nothing."

"Not to me," I whispered. "Now, mate, please put me down and give me that green wand so I can stop worrying about you bleeding to death or getting rabies or something."

"What is rabies?"

"Nevermind. Just...please."

Cormac lowered me to the ground, and I stood before

him with my hand out until he dug around in his suit and produced the healing gadget. He activated it somehow and gave it to me.

"Thank you. Now, sit. Or lay down. I don't care, but I'm using this thing all over you, and I can't reach your head."

My mate went down on one knee like a knight from Camelot and bowed his head so I could reach everywhere.

I moved as slowly as I dared, starting with the nasty furrowed slices on his shoulders and upper arms. Once the wand flashed a different color—which I assumed meant it was done doing whatever it needed to do—I started at the top of his head and covered every inch of him. He was mine, too. I didn't care if he was covered in blood and gore, as long as none of it was his.

His breathing slowed as I worked, and I took that as a good sign until he suddenly reached out and pulled me to him, his head resting dead center in my chest. He stayed there like a little boy who needed comfort, his arms locked around me until one of the Atlans yelled that the ship was ready and it was time to go.

Cormac stood, and I gave him a quick, tight squeeze around his waist before turning to yell at the first Atlan I saw.

"Stryck, come here, please."

The Atlan, still in beast mode, moved with shocking fluidity to stand a few paces in front of me. I looked him over from head to toe. Yep. Covered in blood and guts and god only knew how much of it was his.

"Have a seat, big guy. And hold out those hands." He'd spent who knows how long pounding at his prison cell. I imagined every bone in his hand must have been broken dozens of times.

Stryck did not sit. He knelt on one knee, as Cormac had. And he...shrank. Kind of. His face returned to normal, his body still huge but not *Incredible Hulk* proportions. He held out his hand, first one, then the other. When the light flickered, he moved them around, pulling away when I tried to lift the wand to a nasty-looking cut on his head. Instead, he inclined his head to me in a small bow. "Thank you, my lady. The rest of my injuries are minor. Others require your attention first."

Were all aliens this freaking noble and selfless and just...wow. "Okay. Who should I chase down first?"

"Your legs are too short for a hunt. You would catch none of us."

"It's a turn of phrase. Never mind. Who's hurt the worst?"

"The Hyperion."

16

Abby

"*R*uk?" Ruk was hurt? Badly?

I felt Cormac stiffen in alarm and realized I hadn't seen the big guy since he'd peeked his head in the entrance to ask if we were all right. "Where is he?"

"He is already on board the ship. We carried him to the cargo area and covered him in blankets. He wears no armor, and Latiri 4 is cold."

"You aren't wearing armor, either," I pointed out. In fact, he wasn't wearing anything except a pair of ripped pants. I wasn't dead. Nine super-sized, gorgeous men—aliens, don't forget they are aliens—with more muscles than seemed right or fair? And all on display? At the moment, I had my own professional, nearly naked basketball team. Except bigger. And taller. Some darker skinned. Some light. All magnificent.

And I didn't want any of them. Not like that. I was a one man kind of girl. My man.

"Okay. Take us to him, please." I glanced back over my shoulder at Cormac. I was more than willing to help these guys heal, but I was still too rattled by nearly being eaten alive by those scary black scaly dog monsters to let my mate out of my sight. I needed him next to me, or I wouldn't feel safe. At all. "Will you come with me?"

Cormac snorted as if I had asked the most ridiculous question ever spoken. Even Stryck grinned, a bloody, feral thing on his face. He was so terrifying and so adorable all at once that no words would form in my mouth. These guys were just like the Atlans on Earth. Heartbreakers, every one of them.

Stryck led the way. I followed of my own accord until I stumbled, just a bit, over a rock I hadn't seen. The next instant Cormac was carrying me again. I was tired and scared and grateful that he was mine.

Ruk was in worse shape than any of the Atlans. He was lying on his back near a wall in the cargo area of the Hive ship. I knelt beside him with the wand and started on the multitude of cuts I could see on his face. Based on Cormac's wounds, I figured they would only take a few seconds to close, and I thought it might be nice for Ruk to have at least one place on his body that didn't hurt.

He watched me with quiet eyes, but neither spoke nor made any protest. Face as good as I could get it without being able to see through the dried blood, I reached for his hand and gave it a gentle squeeze. "I'm going to pull the blanket down now and take a look at you. Okay?"

It seemed like he nodded. I wasn't sure. But he squeezed my hand, so I knew he heard me.

Shaking, I peeled the blanket down his body, from chin to hip bones—I didn't dare go lower, not yet. Tears clogged my throat as I took in the criss-cross of raw, gaping wounds on his chest. "What did you do to yourself?"

Cormac got down on the floor next to me to inspect the damage up close. "He defeated at least twelve Hive Soldiers and twice as many of the creatures who tried to kill you."

"What?" I looked down at Ruk, knowing my shock would show clearly on my face. I did nothing to hide it. "No wonder you look like shit," I said as I lowered the wand to the widest of the gaping wounds.

Ruk's chest began to shake up and down. Scowling now, I looked into his face again. "Hold still, you maniac. I'm trying to help you."

The shaking grew worse, and I waved the healing wand to and fro, trying to get the glowing green end as close to the wound as possible.

"Stop moving. I'm serious. You are not going to die, so knock it off and hold still."

Low, rumbling laughter echoed through the cargo area. Apparently, he found something about this bloody mess amusing.

"Cormac?" he said.

"I'm here. You really should hold still. You've lost a lot of blood." My mate placed his hand gently on his friend's shoulder, and I started there. Maybe Cormac could hold at least one part of this stubborn alien still.

"What planet is your mate from?"

"Earth," I said.

"Coalition Fleet maps know the planet as Sol, Terra 3. But the humans call their planet Earth."

What? Earth wasn't the name of Earth?

Ruk closed his eyes and relaxed like he was in a deep sleep, so I dropped that thought and got to work. I should have known the alien couldn't stay quiet for long.

"I should like to visit this Earth. Are there more females like you?" Ruk asked.

It was my turn to snort. "Billions."

The grin on his face never faded over the next hour as I worked. When I was done, he was asleep. Cormac had to help me stand. My feet had gone numb and tingled as they tried to come back to life. My back ached from leaning over Ruk for so long, and my knees felt like I'd tried to do hours of yoga on a hard floor with no mat.

I leaned into him, content when his arm settled around my waist, and his hand came to rest on my hip. He felt like home already.

With a sigh full of regret, I pulled away. "Okay. Who's next?"

"Where is he?" A loud shout sounded from the corridor outside where we stood. Seconds later, an unfamiliar male burst into the room. He was big, but not as big as Cormac or the Atlans, but still well built. He had dark brown hair with an attractive amount of stubble, piercing green eyes and the bits of his skin I could see on his neck were covered with tattoos of...names? He had fangs, as did the silver-haired alien who stomped in behind him. This one had hair so pale it looked silver. It was long and woven into a braid that somehow made him look sexier. They stopped cold in their tracks when they caught sight of Cormac and me.

"What the fuck happened to you?" The dark-haired one demanded. He was glaring at Cormac. The look he was giving my mate made me mad. So I stepped in front of Cormac and glared right back.

Don't do it, Abby. Don't do it.

Shit. I'd never been much good at controlling my tongue with my father. Why should I start now? This guy —whoever the hell he thought he was—was *not* going to yell at Cormac like that again.

"Are you blind? I would think the ground outside would provide the answer to that question. Cormac and the others took out two ships full of Hive."

The two males shifted their attention from Cormac to me. The silver-haired hunk spoke first. "No doubt. She's human, all right."

"What is that supposed to mean?" I asked. What was their problem?

The dark-haired male stared at me with intense green eyes—unnaturally green, like white frosting mixed with a few drops of food coloring. I would not look away. Cormac was mine and I was his. If he could battle those Hive things to protect me, I could stare down a rude stranger.

The staring contest lasted just a few seconds before he smiled. "Our mate, Harper, is also from Earth. I am Styx, Cormac's brother. This is Blade."

Oh. Oops. "Nice to meet you. I'm Abigail Gregg. But you can call me Abby."

"Welcome to Styx legion, Abby. And welcome to my family."

Family? I had a whole family now?

Styx nodded his head and looked at Cormac. "Fuck, brother. You had me worried." He moved forward and grabbed Cormac—gore and all—in a tight embrace. "By the gods, it's good to see you."

Cormac looked dazed. Surprised? I couldn't tell exactly what was going on in his head. I decided I'd ask him later.

Blade stepped forward to introduce himself. He was like a mythical being, oddly beautiful with gray eyes that looked like polished steel. He turned back and yelled over his shoulder. "All right, Harper. It's safe."

And there in the doorway was a woman. From Earth. Just like me. Blonde. She was a lot taller than me and a lot curvier, and she had green eyes instead of blue, but the mere sight of her made me tear up. She ran toward me and hugged me like we had been best friends for years and years.

"Oh my god! Another Earth girl! Ivy is going to be so excited."

"Who's Ivy?"

"Now there will be three of us! And you're my sister! Well, sister-in-law, but that's sisters, right?" She squeezed me until I couldn't breathe, then let go just as abruptly. "Okay. Where is he?" She turned to me with a quick explanation. "I was a nurse back home. Now I'm one of the legion's experts with these bad boys." She waved a larger green wand than the one I'd been using. That one would heal a larger area much faster.

Thank god, because Ruk did not look good. At all. And his chest was rattling with every breath as if he had fluid—or blood—in his lungs.

Harper zeroed in on him at once and dropped to her knees. Her quick, efficient inspection of his body left me absolutely convinced she'd told the truth. Medical personnel had an almost brutal way of looking at things like Ruk's wounds. She tried to get him to speak, looked in his eyes and pressed on his body in multiple places as we all watched in silence.

"What the hell did you do to yourself?" Her whispered question was full of worry, which made me nervous. She looked at her mates. "He needs a ReGen pod. I can keep him breathing, but I can't save him. Not with this." She lifted the large green device to show her mates and then turned back to her patient. "Is there a pod on this ship?"

"No." Enzo walked into the space and the cargo area

—full of five standing alien warriors—suddenly felt like a coat closet. "We have completed our inspection. The ship is in excellent condition, but there is no medical station."

Styx frowned. "Of course not. Their fighters are expendable. They will just make more. Fucking bastards."

"Well, we need to find one, or he's going to die," Harper insisted.

I walked up to stand beside her. "I have this one. It's small, but it might help."

She indicated that I should take up a position near Ruk's head. "Good. Just keep it on his head. If we're lucky, it will be able to help with his brain bleed."

"Brain bleed?" Not good. Not good at all. I held my green wand over his head with absolute conviction. I was not moving a muscle, not if I was the only thing stopping his brain injury from killing him.

17

Cormac, Rogue 5, Styx Legion, Medical Center

hree days Ruk had been unconscious in the ReGen pod. Three days my mate sat by his side until I came to retrieve her. The other members of the legion did not know what to think about my quiet little human, nor about the Hyperion on Rogue 5. The legions of Rogue 5 were descendants of the Hyperion bloodlines. Some of us, like me, would occasionally visit the planet. The Hyperions, however, never came to this moon.

Until we'd brought Ruk home and placed him in that pod. I had no idea what he was going to want to do when he woke up. We had sent word to his clan, filling them in on what had happened.

His father and the other warriors were hunting for a traitor.

As was I.

Abby glanced up when I entered the room. As always, she held out her hand to me and I fought disbelief that she was really mine. "He still isn't awake. All the Atlans are out."

"Much to my brother's chagrin."

Abby grinned up at me. "Stirring up trouble, are they?"

"You could say that." Styx and the others weren't having an issue with the Atlans so much as with the willing females of Styx legion who had not yet chosen a mate. The Atlans had set up a repair bay to tear apart and rebuild the Hive ship they'd taken. I didn't know exactly what they were doing, nor did I care. They had helped save Abby's life. They could take ten ships if they wanted to.

Abby's expression darkened quickly as she looked over her shoulder at Ruk's still form beneath the translucent cover. "Why isn't he waking up?"

I moved to her side and wrapped my warm hand around her chilled fingers. "He is Hyperion. The ReGen tech will work, but it hasn't been tuned to his physiology. They have been perfected for members of the Coalition of Planets. Hyperion is not one of them."

"Well, I don't like it. I'm worried."

"Do not worry. I will have the doctor speak to you again if necessary. I will not allow you to suffer."

She chuckled at me and looked up with a smile on her face. "You cannot order me to stop worrying. And I know what the doctor said. I don't need to talk to her again."

Gently, I pulled her to her feet and wrapped her in my arms. She melted against me, accepting and soft. She'd said she loved me. I didn't quite believe it, but I wasn't sure I knew how love would feel. All I knew was that I did not want to live a day without her. Not one fucking day. She was everything. My life. My heart. My reason to hunt. And kill.

Someone had sold our armor technology to the Hive. Someone was organizing the kidnapping and transport of native Hyperions to Hive integration centers. Someone had tried to kill me and as many members of Styx legion as possible with a bomb planted on Styx's personal ship. Someone had access to the docking bays at Transport Station Zenith.

Someone had nearly murdered my mate.

Every cell in my body burned with rage at the thought. No matter how long the hunt lasted, I would find this someone and dismember him. Rip his head from his body and leave any others in league with him a message. Go after my mate, me, or my legion and die a brutal, hideous, merciless death.

Head resting on my chest, Abby sighed. "Are you done with all of your legion business?"

"Almost. Are you hungry?"

"Yes." She looked up at me, desire making her eyes

dark. She licked her lips and I nearly groaned. "But not for food."

I lifted both hands to her head and held her in place for my kiss. I took her lips with a hunger I knew would never fade. She submitted at once, her body soft and pliant as she wrapped her arms around my neck and pressed close.

My cock had hardened the moment I'd seen her. Always, I wanted her.

Unfortunately, the legion had plans for us tonight.

I pulled away and leaned my forehead down to touch hers. The intimacy of the act had made this closeness one of my favorites. "I will pleasure you tonight, mate. Right now, the legion waits for us."

"What does that mean?"

"Come. You will see."

Taking her hand I escorted her to the large gathering area in the center of Styx territory.

We walked into the area through a side entrance and Abby stopped dead in her tracks. "What is this?"

At the sound of her voice, complete silence fell over those assembled.

There, on a raised stage stood Styx, Harper and Blade along with the other Enforcers, Silver, Ivar and Kohn. Standing at attention in front of the stage stood two rows made up of five captains and ten lieutenants. My captains. My lieutenants. Behind them, the legion. Men, women and children. Waiting. Low murmurs of talking and laughter stopped but we had both heard the space filled with happy noise.

Standing center stage was our elder, Scribe. The title handed down for generations to the male or female who kept the legions records, served as a personal advisor to Styx and did all of the tattoo work for our people.

"Come, mate. It is time to meet your new family." I led my mate up onto the stage and walked to stand before Scribe. Abby looked around, clearly confused until I removed my shirt and bared my chest. "Scribe, this is my mate, Abigail. I would have her name mark my flesh."

Abby gasped. "But I thought you only added members of your legion. I'm not. I mean, I want to be, but I'm not yet. Am I?"

Styx walked forward and removed his shirt as well. "Scribe, please add my new sister, Abigail, to the names of those I care for and protect. I declare Abigail one of us, mate to Cormac, my sister."

The people behind the captains and lieutenants cheered and shouted encouragement as Scribe found my name on Styx's body and added Abigail's next to it in slightly smaller letters. My brother was covered in ink, thousands of names. He didn't have a lot of room left. I approved, glad the legion was so welcoming to her, but the letters were too small.

Like my brother, my body was covered with names. Styx and our parents who had taken me in when I had no one. Harper and Blade, my brother's chosen family. The names of the other enforcers and those of the captains and lieutenants who served under me, part of the system of trade and protection that made our legion strong.

One name was missing, had always been missing. Hers.

Abby was wiping away tears when Styx stood. He walked to her and kissed her on the forehead.

"Welcome, sister. You are one of us now."

"Thank you."

Harper stepped forward to hug my mate as Scribe turned to me with a question in his eyes.

Grinning, I placed my entire palm flat over the bare skin just above my heart. I'd left that place—the traditional skin saved for a mate's name—blank out of pure, stupid hope.

Scribe lifted the hand in which he held the marking device but I grabbed his wrist before he could begin.

"Make my mate's mark on me as large as possible." I wanted everyone to know I belonged to her, heart and soul, from across the room. Fuck that, from the other side of moon. Mine. She was mine.

Scribe cackled with glee and got to work.

"Cormac!" Abby protested. "Doesn't that hurt?"

I grinned back at her as Scribe started on the second letter. When he was done, Abby walked to me and placed her palm over her name. Well, over some of it. Her small hand was not big enough to cover it completely. "I love you, Cormac."

The crowd who had been cheering and shouting

encouragement went silent. My mate seemed to have that effect on everyone and not just me.

Abby turned away from me and looked out at all those strange faces. "What? You never hear anyone say *'I love you'* before?"

Clear as a bell a child shouted back, "Not to him!"

Gut wrenching pain sliced through my happiness like a blade through water. How had I forgotten my place here? I was the monster they all feared. Their killer. Their assassin. Their protector. They needed me. They feared me. They did not care for me.

With my face heated and dread a pit in my gut, I waited for my mate's reaction. I had warned her what I was to my people. What I had done. She was young and vibrant, filled with life. I was too old, had done too much killing.

Abby removed her hand from my chest and it took every ounce of self-control I possessed not to react to the loss. When she stepped in front of me, hands on her hips, I had no idea what was going to come out of her mouth.

"Shame on you. All of you!" She shouted at my legion like a mother scolding small children. "He protects you. He kills your enemies so you can sleep at night and not worry about your children. He has to be big and scary and mean to take care of you. All of you. How dare you treat him like an outsider?"

The silence stretched and Styx stepped forward to announce our mating feast.

Abby snorted, turned around and grabbed my hand.

Pulling me off the stage she asked Harper to point in the direction of the food. Beneath her breathe she mumbled.

"Idiots."

Shock turned my mind to sludge as she dragged me toward the door. Then...

I burst into laughter. Loud. Carefree. Not caring who watched, I pulled her into my arms and kissed her with everything I was. My heart was hers. My soul. My happiness.

"I love you, Abby. My heart is yours."

Abby leaned close and I bent to give her my ear so she could whisper to me.

"Right now, lover boy, I want food. And then we are going to forget about all of these stupid, ungrateful people and get naked."

Perfect. My mate was fucking perfect.

~

*A*bby

*M*y mind was an endless stream of insults. I wanted to like these people, I really did. They weren't making it easy.

I sat with Cormac on a large bench placed along the far wall of the celebration area. The main dining hall they all used for most meals wasn't large enough to hold everyone at once, so they'd pulled the seating and put it out in the street. If this was a street.

I'd never been on an alien home base before.

Scratch that for a lie, but I refused to count Latiri 4 and the Hive base. That place was for war, a prison, not a home.

The dome sky looked brighter than I'd imagined it would. It wasn't blue like the sky at home, but it was a bit blue and silver. Pretty even if unfamiliar. The buildings were not more than three or four stories tall, but they stretched in every direction, clean, well-kept streets between them that buzzed with small vehicles that gave it the energy of a mid-sized city. Color was everywhere. The base color of everything was silver, which I assumed was because this was Styx territory and their legion's mark was silver. But on top of that, painted in giant swaths was every color imaginable. Cheerful lights hung in strings between buildings. The place was lit up like a Christmas tree.

Some musicians played nearby; happy dancing music made my foot tap in time to the music even as I scowled at everyone who dared look our way.

These people made me mad. Not just angry, furious. Cormac had tried to tell me but I thought he was exaggerating or reading the situation incorrectly. But no. They were all afraid of him and they treated him like a monster, not a person.

"How long do we have to stay here?" I leaned against Cormac's side, my head resting on his upper arm.

Cormac sighed, a sound I rarely heard from him. "Harper put a lot of work into this celebration."

"And if we leave early, we'll hurt her feelings."

"Yes."

That was my big, mean monster, worried about his sister-in-law's feelings. I slid my hand beneath his elbow where it rested on his thigh and laced my fingers with his. "Okay. Just tell me when it's been long enough. I want you to myself." Cormac had said he loved me—in front of *everyone.* No one had ever claimed me like that, publicly, not caring who was watching or who might judge him or cancel a business deal. I craved him like a starving woman craved chocolate. I *needed* to touch him, to have him touch me. I needed his skin on my skin and his cock filling me up. I just needed *him.*

From the corner of my eye I saw a small girl, perhaps six or seven, approaching us slowly. She would take a few steps, watch, take a few more.

I caught the child's gaze and smiled, waving her closer with my free hand.

Staring at her little feet, the girl—wearing a smaller version of Styx armor with the telltale silver band around her arm—came over and stopped next to me, on the opposite side of Cormac.

"Hello. What's your name?"

When the girl remained mute, Cormac answered for her. "This little one is Amora. She is the daughter of one of my captains." He softened his voice. "She has a baby brother named Lorn, and, I believe, she has a birthing day celebration coming very soon."

Amora looked up at Cormac and smiled, her shyness forgotten. "My mama is making me my favorite treats and I have two friends staying at our home *overnight*!"

Adorable, that's what she was. And of course Cormac knew her name, her baby brother's name and who her parents were. Some monster.

"I, ummm—" she looked down at her hand and I noticed she held something there that looked like a piece of paper. "I am supposed to give this message to Cormac but I don't want you to be mad at me because I'm not supposed to talk to them."

"To who, honey?" I asked.

"Siren. He said you're even now." She moved her hand in a horizontal slash. "Like this. Even. He had a red arm band, but he was really nice. He said he's an Enforcer just like you."

Siren? Wasn't that one of the other legions?

Cormac stilled into what I was beginning to recognize as his Enforcer, hunter-protector mode. He held out his hand and placed his palm up in front of the little girl. His voice was soft and friendly, gentler than I'd ever heard him. "It's all right, little one. Give me the message."

Biting her lower lip, she stepped forward and placed her small hand in the center of Cormac's much larger one. She unfolded her fingers and a small, crinkled piece of gray paper fell free.

"Thank you," Cormac said.

The little girl looked at me. "I don't want you to be mad at me, either."

"I'm not mad at you, Amora. Everything is fine."

She studied me for long moments, her little mind obviously churning over something she found very important. Decision made, she turned to Cormac, walked straight into his body and wrapped her tiny arms around him the best she could. "I decided to tell you that I'm not afraid of you anymore."

She clung until he wrapped his free arm—the hand still holding the note—around her and hugged her close. "I am glad."

"Can we be friends?"

"Yes."

She smiled and pulled back. "Good. I don't want to fight the bad people."

"Never. I promise. I will always protect you."

Filled with glee at Cormac's promise she hopped up and down, clapped her hands and darted away.

18

Cormac

I knew exactly which member of Siren had dared sneak into Styx territory. Shade. I'd allowed him to live and now, apparently, he decided to repay the favor.

Or save his legion. My brother had already requested a formal meeting with Siren in the neutral territory. If Styx didn't get the answers he wanted from her—specifically the names and heads of whoever in her legion was responsible for Ruk's condition as well as the stolen tech they'd sold to the Hive—there would be a lot of blood spilled in the coming weeks. I knew much of the death would be by my hand.

Abby watched the little girl as she walked away and the softness in her gaze made me dare ask a question I had held back until now. I still struggled to accept she was mine. I did not need more. Whatever she wanted I would give to her.

"Do you wish to have children, mate?"

She jumped as if I'd poked her then laughed. "Not right now. But yes. Maybe in a few years? Do you want a family?" Her small fingers squeezed my hand where I held hers. I'd been touching her every moment I could, grounding myself in her peace, reminding myself that we were alive and well. Home.

"I want you." Leaning down I whispered the next bit into her ear. "I want what you want, female. I need you to be happy. Food. Children. No children. Orgasms. Anything, mate. Ask and I will provide."

Her face turned that delightful shade of pink I had not seen since we'd left Transport Station Zenith. "Cormac!" She smacked my chest with her free hand as I nibbled on her neck. My fangs were throbbing, eager to sink into her soft flesh as I fucked her with my cock.

Abby turned her head so that our lips touched and I took full advantage, kissing her in front of everyone. I did not care who watched. She was everything I wanted in a mate and she was mine.

With a quiet sigh that made my cock jerk in my pants, she pulled back just far enough to end the kiss. "People are watching us."

"Yes. And now they all know exactly how I feel about you." I kissed her gently, a brushing of lips. "And they know what I will do to them if you are upset or hurt."

"Upset or hurt?" She shook her head. "Women get upset all the time."

"Not my woman."

"You're impossible."

"I am yours."

Her smile made me feel like I had just slayed an entire legion of her enemies. "How can I be irritated when you keep saying things like that?"

"You are not allowed to be irritated with your mate."

She lifted her face to the ceiling and laughed, the sound pure joy. Anyone who had been pretending not to watch our interaction gave up the pretense and stared. I could not blame them. She was beyond lovely.

We settled into a comfortable silence and she squeezed my hand once more. "Cormac, what's in the note?"

I had glanced at the message as Amora walked away. It was short and succinct. "A name."

"A name?"

"Yes. The name of a group within Siren responsible for placing the bomb on my ship. They are also, apparently, the same group who sold our tech to the Hive and have been kidnapping native Hyperions to sell."

"One group of people is doing all of that?"

"Yes."

"How many are there, in this group?"

I had not seen them for some time, but I knew their leader well. He was scum. I should have killed him years ago, but I had followed orders and allowed him to live.

This time, he would not be so lucky. "The last I knew there were seven or eight. I do not know their numbers now."

"What are you going to do?"

"You know the answer to that question, Abby."

"You're going to kill them."

"Yes."

"I don't want you to do that."

There it was, the knife in my heart I'd been waiting for from the moment I met her. She was young and compassionate and innocent. I could not blame her for not wanting to be mated to a killer. "I do what must be done."

"But—"

I released her hand and stood, catching my brother's eye as I did so. He would know what the nearly imperceptible tilt of my head meant. I walked away without a backward glance, fearless in the face of our enemies. Terrified of what I might see if I looked back at hers.

Styx followed me out of the community area to weapon storage. He arrived as I entered the security code that would open the door.

"I saw Shade speaking to Amora. Did he give us what we need?"

"Yes." I walked inside and pulled two blades free from the wall. I added an ion blaster as well, even though I had to assume they would be wearing the same advanced armor that would make the weapon useless. "Did you send word to Commander Karter about the base on

Latiri 4 as well as the new armor the Hive have acquired?"

"I did." Styx groaned as he pulled his own set of blades from the walls. "He took the news well, considering."

"You did not tell him about the Atlans."

"Of course not. As we agreed."

"Good. I would not want Abby upset with you." I grinned as I changed out of my civilian clothing into my hunting armor. "I would have to kick your ass to make her happy."

My brother laughed. "You can try, brother. We have not tested your ability to beat me since I was eight and you fifteen. If I recall, I kicked your ass even then."

It was my turn to chuckle. What he said was true. But I had allowed him to best me and we both knew it. That fact had not prevented him from using it against me every chance he got.

We prepared in silence. I had known he would come with me, not as the leader of our legion, but as my brother. I was surprised, however, when the other Enforcers walked in and began suiting up as well. Blade, Silver, Kohn and Ivar changed quickly, their faces grim.

Silver, Blades equally deadly sister, finished preparing first. "So, scum hunting tonight?"

"Yes," I replied.

"And our blasters won't work because they stole our tech?"

"Yes."

"And sold it to the Hive?"

"Yes."

"And they've been kidnapping Hyperions and selling them for experiments?"

I shoved a third knife into place in the holster on my left leg. A fourth on my right. "Yes." I looked up and met the gaze of each of them before continuing. "They tried to kill me and half our legion with that bomb." My voice dropped as I allowed the rage to bubble up from the deep well within me. "They nearly killed my mate."

Silver smiled at me, which would have been lovely on any other female. On her it was a threat. "Understood. You do your thing, and we'll work clean-up."

I nodded and led the way out the door. I knew exactly where these fuckers had their safe houses in the neutral territory. Their location would not save them tonight. I would bathe in their blood and pray my mate could forgive me.

wo Hours Later

he threat to Abby had been eliminated. As promised Silver and the others had followed me to finish off anyone I missed.

I left them nothing, my rage at the threat to Abby so

complete I was worse than an Atlan in beast mode. I ripped limbs from their bodies, stomped skulls into paste and when I had found their leader, I had tortured him until he gave us the name of the individual he used to contact the Hive. To my surprise, his contact was a member of the Coalition Fleet. According to my new source, the male was a spy and thief for the Silver Scions, a group that dealt exclusively in illegal Hive tech. Hive ships. Engines. Weapons. Even upgrades for the body, super-strong limbs or brain chips. Everything they did made them a target of the Interstellar Coalition of Planets.

That information would go to the Coalition as well, for the right price. Styx and I knew a certain member of their Intelligence Core who was as ruthless about protecting his people as I. Doctor Helion would hunt the traitor down without mercy and destroy anyone and everyone he even suspected of participating. I knew from experience that the Prillon would pay well for valuable information such as this.

However, the Coalition was not my concern. Which meant I could rest now. Go back to my life protecting my legion, hunting our enemies and fucking my female.

If she would have me.

'I don't want you to do that.'

She had not spoken such words to me before our battle with the Hive. But the Hive were not people, they were automations controlled by a Hive mind. The Siren males I had torn into pieces this day had screamed with their own lungs, acted with their own fear. Died for their betrayal.

Styx walked next to me, shoulder to shoulder as we had for as long as I could remember. The others looked relatively clean for just having been in a fight. I was unrecognizable, covered head to toe in blood. They had kept their word and stayed the fuck out of my way.

We walked, as a unit, through the busiest sections of the neutral zone. Styx wanted everyone to know what betraying our legion would cost them. Word would travel quickly, further cementing our reputation as a strong, merciless, not-to-be-fucked-with legion on Rogue 5. We and Kronos were the two strongest legions and could wipe out the others if we so chose. I was the monster that scared the children and Styx used my infamy to our legion's advantage. I made sure to keep my countenance severe as we walked past gaping males and females, children shouting and pointing, running to collect their friends so they, too, could see the parade of blood with me at its head.

At the rear was a hovering cargo crate stacked with Siren dead. When we reached the center of the busy territory, we dropped the bodies on the ground in a heap and Styx stepped forward.

"I am Styx. Hear me Rogue 5. Siren legion has stolen our technology and sold it to the Hive. They are kidnapping native Hyperions, carriers of our ancestral bloodlines, and selling them to Hive Integration Units for experimentation and torture. And they tried to kill me, my brother and many members of my legion. You see their fate. We will show no mercy to anyone else involved and offer a reward for any information that will lead us to their accomplices. We are Styx."

A nervous hush lingered after Styx finished shouting his speech. He led the rest of our team away, taking the now empty cargo crate with him. I, however, walked around the bodies one last time inspecting my work. Satisfied, I glanced up to find a male from Siren legion staring at me. "Do you know who I am, Siren?"

"Yes."

"What is my name?"

"Cormac."

I nodded my head. "You tell that bitch you call a leader if she fucks with Styx again, I am coming for her head."

He swallowed slowly and nodded his head. Satisfied my message would be delivered, if not by him than by one of the dozens of others standing around gawking, I walked away.

I was done. Abby was safe. Styx would figure out what to do about the rest. I was a weapon, not the leader of our people. I needed everyone on this moon to fear me, all but one.

Abby.

I buried the pain rising to choke me as I caught up to the others. We returned to Styx territory to find the feast still going. The others picked up their pace. When I lingered, Styx dropped back to speak with me.

"What are you doing?"

"I cannot allow Abby to see me like this."

"It is who you are."

"She will reject me, brother. She told me not to do this, not to kill, and I walked away from her."

My brother slapped me on the back, then wiped his blood covered hand on his armored thigh. "She is yours, Cormac. Trust in that."

He left me alone in the corridor, looking in through a window as our people laughed and danced and feasted without a care. My gaze found Abby at once. She was sitting at a table across from Harper. Their hands touched on top of the table and they looked to be deep in conversation. Seated around them like a security detail were the nine Atlans we had rescued on Latiri 4. Their loyalty to my mate obvious in the way they kept close to her and continued to scan the crowd for imminent threats.

Good. I approved. Although it required nine beasts to replace me.

I saw the moment Harper looked up and caught sight of her mates, Styx and Blade. She jumped to her feet and ran to them, throwing her arms around them and kissing them both in turn as our legion cheered.

The rest of the team was greeted with loud cries of congratulations and slaps on the back.

From my place just outside the window, my gaze drifted back to Abby. She rose slowly, a look of confusion on her face. She scanned the team, looking for something.

Looking for me.

I looked down at my blood-soaked body and sighed. This was who I was. I fought. I killed. I protected my people. I protected *her*. Perhaps she would be upset with me, but I had to believe that with time—and a lot of orgasms—I could convince her to ignore the dark side of me and stay.

I needed her to stay. To choose me.

Fuck. I was in love with her. I loved her. Totally and completely. Losing her would destroy me.

Braced for the worst, I opened the door and walked into the room. Gasps came from several directions. Everyone froze, staring at what had to be a monstrous visage. I did not believe there was a single part of me not covered in blood, imagined my eyes as two bright orbs staring at the assembled crowd. I truly was a thing of nightmares.

Abby's cry was the loudest. "Oh my god! Cormac?" She ran in my direction but stopped several paces in front of me.

I stood in silence as the entire legion watched our interaction. I could not speak over the lump of pain clogging my throat. I had expected this reaction. I had underestimated how much her rejection would hurt.

"Are you hurt? Is any of that blood yours?"

I stared into her crystal blue eyes and spoke the truth. "No. I am covered in the blood of your enemies."

"Thank god!" She ran to me and leaped, her arms locking behind my neck as she pressed her body fully to mine. "Holy shit. Don't scare me like that!"

"Mate, I—"

"No. No talking. You need a shower. You're getting all those nasty traitors off you, right now." She squeezed me as tightly as I imagined her slight arms could manage without a single care for her own clothing. She dropped to the floor and took my hand. "Come on. Let's go. This party is over for you, mister."

Stunned, I allowed my small mate to pull me along wherever she wanted me to go. I caught Styx's eye as Abby pulled me toward the door. He lifted a glass in salute, the look on his face smug.

Gods be damned, that bastard was always right. Abby had not rejected me, did not hate me. She *worried* about me.

19

Cormac

*a*bby took me to our quarters, stopping just outside the door. She gave me a once over and shook her head. "Nope. That mess is not going inside."

I agreed. Had I not been with her I would have showered in the fighters' area and left the armor to be cleaned by Styx's finely trained crew. "I can go take care of this elsewhere."

"Not what I meant." She glanced down at herself and grimaced. "Gross. This has to go, too."

I had no idea what my mate intended until she reached for the bottom of her shirt and pulled it off over her head. Stunned, I watched her drop it on the floor and reach for the fastening of her pants. We were alone in the corridor, but this was not the place to disrobe. "What are you doing, female?"

"Stripping. Get busy. Take if off. All of it."

"I do not understand. I will go remove this offensive armor and return to you when I am clean."

Abby paused her movement with both hands at her waist, ready to pull her pants off her body. I very much wanted her pants gone. I wanted to touch, taste and lick those breasts, that soft skin. I needed to bury my cock so deep in her eager pussy she begged for more.

"Let me put this another way, *mate*."

Her emphasis on the last word was not lost on me.

"I want to play a game with you. It's called *the naked game*. We take off all our clothes, leave them out here and then we wash each other in the shower."

My cock hardened to the point of pain. And still, I did not move. "I am covered in blood and death. How can you suggest such a thing when I stand before you like this?"

Stepping forward, she reached for the bottom of my armor and tugged until I gave in and helped her. She was much too small to lift the offensive garment over my head. She dropped the blood-soaked garment on top of her own, making an even bigger mess on the floor.

"Don't you get it, Cormac? I don't care about what's on the outside. I only care about what's in here." She placed her palm flat over my bare chest. "Somebody has to kill the bad guys. If no one did, they'd ruin everything, everywhere and hurt a lot of people." She stepped forward and pressed her naked chest to mine, skin to skin, and wrapped her arms around me. "You are one of the good guys, Cormac. That's why I love you."

I grabbed her face, lifting her chin so I could kiss her. And kiss her. I didn't care who saw us, who judged us, who frowned or who smiled in our direction. Did not fucking care. Abby was mine. She had, by some fucking miracle, fallen in love with me. I was brutal and merciless with my enemies, but I was no idiot. I'd been given a gift by Fate or the gods, destiny or the universe, perhaps by sheer dumb luck.

I wasn't giving her back.

I released her and reached for my own pants. "I will play this naked game with you, mate."

Her breathing was ragged and she seemed a bit unsteady after my kisses, but she grinned and tugged at her own pants. We were both bare faster than I'd thought possible, our clothing two forgotten heaps on the floor. I opened the door to our quarters and gently smacked Abby's ass when she streaked past me, headed for the bathing room.

"Cormac!"

"Yes?"

"Behave."

"Why would I do that?"

She smiled and turned on the spray of warm water, beckoning to me to join her. I did so and she told me to get down on my knees.

"Why?"

"So I can wash your hair."

I sank to my knees and allowed my mate to have her way with me. She ran warm water through my hair, added cleanser and massaged my scalp in circular motions. She used a soft cleansing cloth on my face, paying attention to detail, trailing kisses over my forehead, cheeks and jaw as she wiped away all traces of my activities that day. She took special care with my hands, lifting my palms to kiss them once they were spotless. She took her time, touching me everywhere, caring for me. No one had ever shown me such tenderness. I protected my brother and my legion. I took care of myself. Had since I was a child little older than the girl, Amora.

I thought perhaps I should pull her close and ravish her, make her come with my tongue in her pussy, make her scream as she orgasmed around my cock. I wanted that. Badly.

But I needed this more.

Something inside me broke wide open as she touched me, soothed me. Pain exploded from the wound I'd buried inside my soul like flames shooting from a star. The hurt was indescribable, and yet I could not move away. My body locked in place. I was hers to touch, to tend to, to love.

This agony burning my soul to ash was love.

She traced the lines of her name on my skin and I stared up into her eyes. Everything I was feeling I saw reflected there. "I am yours. Your mate. Your protector. You are my heart, Abby."

This time it was her hands on the sides of my face, her leaning down to steal a kiss. "I'm not going anywhere. And I'm not letting you go."

My body ached for her. My cock was a rigid torment by the time she leaned over to turn off the warm water. Unable to deny either of us another moment, I cupped her pussy from behind. I groaned when wet welcome instantly coated my palm. She froze, completely at my mercy. I took the opportunity to slide two fingers into her from behind.

"This is not how the game is supposed to go," she panted. "We're supposed to get dried off and then do this in bed."

"Played before, have you?"

"No."

"Neither have I." I lifted her in my arms and pressed her back to the wall. "I can't wait for you, mate. I need to fuck you now."

"Yes." She wrapped her legs around my hips and reached low to place my cock at the entrance to her tight pussy.

Not needing more of an invitation, I held her in place and moved slowly, taking my time, enjoying the tight fist of her pussy taking me deep, filling the broken pieces inside me with her acceptance. Her forgiveness. For knowing what I was, what I had been, and loving the dark, twisted pieces of my soul.

bby

$\mathcal{I}$'d nearly burst into tears at the surprised bliss on Cormac's face when I had bathed him. He'd moaned with what sounded like pain as I'd washed his hair. I took the time to rub his scalp and make sure every microscopic molecule of those bastards was gone. Rinsed clean. Erased.

I didn't want that evil touching him for one second longer than necessary.

He'd been almost hypnotized by my touch, the power to give him such pleasure a heady sensation. One I'd never experienced before. I'd been treated like a princess my entire life, pampered and paid off, given every material thing I'd ever asked for. Denied the one thing I needed.

This.

Connection.

Cormac's skin on mine. The longing on his face. Feeling wanted. Needed. Loved.

I took his face in my hands, leaned over just a bit, and kissed him until I couldn't breathe, couldn't think. Until there was only him.

"I can't wait for you, mate. I need to fuck you now." The deep rumble of his voice made my knees weak.

"Yes." Hell yes. Yes, please. Now. I wanted his cock inside me making me forget my own name. I wanted his fangs buried deep, filling me with bliss. I wanted his skin touching mine, the names marking his flesh moving against me in a reminder of who he was. Powerful. Sexy. Honorable. Safe.

I lifted my legs to his hips and reached between us to guide his cock exactly where I needed him to be. Inside me. Part of me.

My pussy began to spasm as he filled me, stretched me, buried himself deep. I'd waited so long, touched him, wanted him. This was too much. An orgasm built, rising as the bulged head of his cock slipped over the sensitive ridges inside my core. When he was balls deep, he shifted his hips, a mere hint of movement.

Too much.

I exploded in his arms, my teeth biting into his chest where I saw my name. That was *my name* marking his skin. My claim on him. His declaration to me and his legion.

Mine. He really was mine, now. Officially. Publicly.

My bite made his cock jump inside me and he growled into my ear. "Yes. Fuck. Harder."

I used my inner muscles to squeeze his cock and lifted my head to the side, exposing the overheated skin of my neck for his pleasure. "Bite me, mate. Fuck me. Make me come."

He moved like a predator, driving his fangs deep in one frenzied movement.

His name was a low moan in my throat as my pussy spasmed around his cock and my body filled with his essence, a special brand of fire. Better than any drug, any high. His bite was ecstasy.

He moved hips and legs as his essence entered my body. His rhythm changed, all control gone as he pounded in and out of my pussy without mercy.

I needed none. Shouting his name, I came again, my core so sensitive and swollen another wave built immediately. I crashed and burned and gave him everything. I knew he would hold me, protect me, want me and keep me safe. I knew he was truly mine.

Forever.

Ready for more? Read Bachelor Beast next!

Warlord Wulf thought nothing could be worse than being tortured and contaminated by the Hive. That was before he's ordered to transport to Earth and represent The Colony in an unfamiliar horror... a human reality show. The Bachelor Beast is the hottest new program on Earth, but being set up with two dozen clingy females is not his idea of a good time. When his Beast refuses to show the slightest interest in any of the show's potential mates, he knows he must choose one or die due to his raging mating fever.

His Beast prefers execution to claiming anyone but his true mate. Wulf is resigned to his fate, a one-way trip to Atlan, a prison cell and execution. It is the only honorable thing left to do.

Until one glance, one sweet, feminine scent lingering in the air and his beast rages for a female who is not supposed to be his.

But try telling that to his Beast when his entire body transforms on live television and one simple word thunders from his lips...MINE.

Click here to read Bachelor Beast now!

A SPECIAL THANK YOU TO MY READERS...

Want more? I've got *hidden* bonus content on my web site *exclusively* for those on my mailing list.

If you are already on my email list, you don't need to do a thing! Simply scroll to the bottom of my newsletter emails and click on the *super-secret* link.

Not a member? What are you waiting for? In addition to ALL of my bonus content (great new stuff will be added regularly) you will be the first to hear about my newest release the second it hits the stores—AND you will get a free book as a special welcome gift.

Sign up now! http://freescifiromance.com

FIND YOUR INTERSTELLAR MATCH!

YOUR mate is out there. Take the test today and discover your perfect match. Are you ready for a sexy alien mate (or two)?

VOLUNTEER NOW!

interstellarbridesprogram.com

DO YOU LOVE AUDIOBOOKS?

Grace Goodwin's books are now available as audiobooks...everywhere.

LET'S TALK!

Interested in joining my **Sci-Fi Squad**? Meet new like-minded sci-fi romance fanatics and chat with Grace! Get excerpts, cover reveals and sneak peeks before anyone else. Be part of a private Facebook group that shares pictures and fun news! Join here:

https://www.facebook.com/groups/scifisquad/

Want to talk about Grace Goodwin books with others? Join the **SPOILER ROOM** and spoil away! Your GG BFFs are waiting! (And so is Grace) Join here:

https://www.facebook.com/groups/ggspoilerroom/

GET A FREE BOOK!

JOIN MY MAILING LIST TO BE THE FIRST TO KNOW OF NEW RELEASES, FREE BOOKS, SPECIAL PRICES AND OTHER AUTHOR GIVEAWAYS.

http://freescifiromance.com

ALSO BY GRACE GOODWIN

His Virgin Princess

The Virgins - Complete Boxed Set

Interstellar Brides® Program: Ascension Saga

Ascension Saga, book 1

Ascension Saga, book 2

Ascension Saga, book 3

Trinity: Ascension Saga - Volume 1

Ascension Saga, book 4

Ascension Saga, book 5

Ascension Saga, book 6

Faith: Ascension Saga - Volume 2

Ascension Saga, book 7

Ascension Saga, book 8

Ascension Saga, book 9

Destiny: Ascension Saga - Volume 3

Interstellar Brides® Program: The Beasts

Bachelor Beast

Maid for the Beast

Beauty and the Beast

The Beasts Boxed Set

Big Bad Beast

Beast Charming

Bargain with a Beast

ABOUT GRACE

Grace Goodwin is a USA Today and international bestselling author of Sci-Fi and Paranormal romance with over a million books sold. Grace's titles are available worldwide on all retailers, in multiple languages, and in ebook, print, audio and other reading App formats.

Grace is a full-time writer whose earliest movie memories are of Luke Skywalker, Han Solo, and real, working light sabers. (Still waiting for Santa to come through on that one.) Now Grace writes sexy-as-hell sci-fi romance six days a week. In her spare time, she reads, watches campy sci-fi and enjoys spending time with family and friends. No matter where she is, there is always a part of her dreaming up new worlds and exciting characters for her next book.

Grace loves to chat with readers and can frequently be found lurking in her Facebook groups. Interested in joining her **Sci-Fi Squad**? Meet new like-minded sci-fi romance fanatics and chat with Grace! Get excerpts, cover reveals and sneak peeks before anyone else. Join here: https://www.facebook.com/groups/scifisquad/

Want to talk about Grace Goodwin books with others? Join the **SPOILER ROOM** and spoil away! Your GG BFFs are waiting! (And so is Grace) Join here:

https://www.facebook.com/groups/ggspoilerroom/